THE DIARY OF ANNA COMNENA,
OR THE VERY POLITICAL ADVENTURES OF A
TRANSGENDER BYZANTINE PRINCESS IN AFRICAN ELEVATORS

Fig. 1. Hieronymus Bosch, *Ship of Fools* (1490–1500)

First published in 2024 by punctum books, Earth, Milky Way.
https://punctumbooks.com

ISBN-13: 978-1-68571-238-9 (print)
ISBN-13: 978-1-68571-239-6 (ePDF)

DOI: 10.53288/0467.1.00

LCCN: 2024945607
Library of Congress Cataloging Data is available from the Library of Congress

Editing: Vincent W.J. van Gerven Oei and SAJ
Book design: Hatim Eujayl
Cover design: Tis Kaoru Zamler-Carhart and Vincent W.J. van Gerven Oei

HIC SVNT MONSTRA

Tis Kaoru Zamler-Carhart

The Diary of Anna Comnena

or The Very Political Adventures of a Transgender Byzantine Princess in African Elevators

p.

Contents

Acknowledgments

My heartfelt gratitude goes to Amadeus Collins and Andrea Friggi, whose endless generosity with their time and insight allowed this book to take shape, to Samn Johnson, Thomas Langley, Allen W. Strouse, and Louis Bertrand for their steadfast encouragement, to Rahmatou Keïta, Abraham Iradukunda, Elysé Twagirayezu, Abass Kamara, and Ousmane Camara for years of conversation in and about Africa, to Anthony Hirst, Paddy Sammon, and Martine Cuypers of the Byzantine Greek Summer School, to Procopius, Proclus, Porphyry, and Plotinus for teaching me the art of time travel, to Gilles Boucomont for training me in the use of power tools, to my fellow elevator engineers of all countries and centuries, to the many small hands that keep the Byzantine film industry running, to my publisher punctum books for their unfailing support, to Andrew and Vitaly for their indefectible love, and to the angels of the Lord for always showing up on time.

I guess I still dedicate this book to the memory of my father Emperor Alexios I?

I

A Sharp Conical Spike

1

I am Anna Comnena, I'm a Byzantine chronicler, I write about hair.

For example, back in October 1081, hair was in the air. The blond, butch Bohemond of Antioch drubbed my daddy on the battlefield, and it practically rained testosterone for a month after that.

A few years later, hair was in the air again. Daddy was on the throne, I was writing his imperial biography and doing research on the famous hair elevator at the Yamoussoukro basilica in Côte d'Ivoire. I prepared a full engineering report on that elevator, which you'll get in a minute. It's amazing, the place has four hollow pillars that contain all manner of suitable appurtenances for the orderly edification of the faithful,
　like:

— rainwater drain pipes,
— ventilation ducts,
— electrical wiring harnesses,
— sprinkler lines,

all of them shining privately in the dark (like so many of us in fact).

Another two pillars contain elevators. Of these, one is made of hair. Whether it's camel hair or human hair I dare not say, for such speculation is unbecoming of the propriety required by my rank. But it's quite virile.

Daddy is Emperor Alexios, fyi.

I'm his baby, the heir to the throne, born and bred in the Byzantine purple, learned in the art of poetry, economics, elevator engineering, etc., etc., etc. Anyone is welcome to write daddy's imperial biography, but I'm the most qualified.

I write about hair with filial piety, as my lineage demands. I lack Thucydides's golden tongue and Polybius's cunning wit, but I'm very organized. I lack Xenophon's keen eloquence and Strabo's lucid acumen, but I know more than them about elevators. There's a whole lot I lack, but we're also talking about my dad here — men are hard to understand.

Which is why I came up with a practical methodology for my imperial biography project: travel through Africa, educate myself on elevators and other important monuments great macho men have built there, then return to Constantinople with a fresh grasp of the architecture of the cosmos, acclaim my illustrious father's character with due imperial decorum, couple of lines in my chronicle about hair because it's always so masc, and voilà.

I also knew Christ would be with me in this endeavor. At least *he* loves me, his holy spirit would hold my pen even if my own hand should founder, and the many colors of his divine light would diffract through the prism of my poetry even if I should press the wrong button.

So altogether a fail-safe project. Now please join me in the hair elevator for a full report.

In the elevator

The walls were made of coarsely felted hair lined with raspy green corduroy. They buckled and shimmied as I walked in. The ceiling had a mirror rimmed with maroon plastic, the floor a thick foam pad covered in tufted black leatherette. It smelled frisky, like underwear that has been worn for just a few minutes.

By the door was a bronze panel with four knobs. Please refrain from touching any of the knobs, as previous readers have pressed the wrong one before and ended up delaying the story by several pages — thank you.

There was also a faded Manchester United sticker, a pomegranate dispenser, and two masks, which, in this kind of elevator design, typically function as portals to supernatural dimensions. One was a Mossi mask painted dark red with white stripes, with a mane of raffia fibers rilling down from its horns, the other a shiny black Baoulé mask with bulging conical eyes, little crosses carved on its ebony cheeks, and no mouth.

Of course we also have elevators back home in Constantinople, including several in the Blachernae Palace where I grew up. My dad had all of them retrofitted with pomegranate dispensers (my dad loves pomegranates) when I was little.

But — THEY ARE NOT MADE OF HAIR.

I don't know what they're made of, I've never thought about it. But not hair. And if I am to be a loyal child and a faithful biographer, and do justice to the majesty of my father's regal disposition, I need to understand why. Aren't hair elevators more manly, the way hairy chests are more manly?

This brings me to a first point of methodology. As an imperial chronicler, I can get better at recording my father's greatness by studying the character of other great men — elevator builders, religious leaders, television producers, etc. — and paying close attention to how macho their design language is.

In any case, you may step out now, and I will share with you my engineering analysis of our visit to Yamoussoukro's illustrious hair elevator.

"*SIR!*"

I bristled.

"*SIR!*"

The guard approached me. There was nobody else in the whole building.

"*SIR!*"

I ROLLED MY EYES. ~o~O~o~O~o~~~ooOOoo~~~

"It's not allowed to take pictures here, *SIR*," he said.

"hhm**mmm**hm**HHMMmmhm**."

"Thank you, *SIR*."

"mhm."

I took a deep breath, readjusted the wispy yellow cotton whorls around my waist, looked up and out, then remained still like a Byzantine mosaic icon.

"So what do you want?" the guard asked.
    "Hmm?" I muttered.
    "I mean what do you want here, dressed like this in this building?" he asked.
    I shrugged and didn't look at him. Eventually he also shrugged, then turned around and left.

I went outside to catch my breath and walked backward away from the building. I waited for the breeze to blow my dress around my legs and make me feel like Marilyn Monroe.

But it didn't. Yamoussoukro was stupidly hot and windless. I sweated profusely, alone in the vast expanse of the basilica's dusty red esplanade. I finished my bottle of water and felt numb and delirious, as if I was visiting a defunct airport runway dedicated to the glory of God.

Now I've lost my train of thought.

Ah, the elevator.

So yes, the basilica in Yamoussoukro was commissioned by Ivorian president Félix Houphouët-Boigny with money looted from the national treasury. He had ostensibly been a Catholic, but also an animist spirit worshipper — so definitely a man of faith. When he died, hundreds of migrant workers from Burkina Faso were decapitated so his funeral procession could roll by rows of skulls mounted on poles, as befits a great Baoulé chief.

Now let me just say: *that's* super masc. That's some serious daddy vibe right there.

Class warfare is also a nifty resource (just speaking as an engineer now). If you need skulls for a project, you can harvest them from undocumented construction workers. And it's a great way to work across class differences and make it a community project. I ♡ community projects.

Both sides benefitted tbh. For migrant workers, contributing their head to the patriarch's funeral procession was a big career opportunity — once in a lifetime. Besides, John the Baptist had also been decapitated, so even the biblical symbolism worked out tightly. Of course, all large construction sites have labor management issues, and indeed the decapitated workers stuck around and haunt the basilica to this day.

Which brings me to a point of elevator engineering. The two masks are basically just a coin-operated ghost mitigation appliance. They are a tool for labor management, tailored to the unique grievances of a deceased workforce. The Baoulé mask with the conical eyes is a portal to the local spirits of the land under the basilica. Those are earth spirits with no mouths, who mutter in palm fronds and coconut rustles. They are consumer spirits. They have no emotions and no goals. They just want wealth — just to have it.

The Mossi mask is a medium to the murdered migrant workers from Burkina Faso. They mumble in dust and clouds and perpetual motion. They like smoke, smells, air, drifty wafty drafty transient things.

We have a few more important elevators to visit in this imperial chronicle, but not until much later. For now, the takeaway is that great macho men build great things, and that macho engineering seems to involve hair, power, murder, and coin-operated supernatural portals.

I'm conflicted about the supernatural portals, because I don't see where those fit in Byzantine culture. We don't have masks like in Africa, we don't do magic, and we don't interact with spirits *as far as I know.*

But instead of speculating — which is unbecoming of a purple-born Byzantine princess and of the propriety required by my rank — let me distract us with this little poem about coins:

Both masks were operated with

COIN PAYMENTS*

(*the industry standard in Dead Workforce Mediation)

coins went in a
little hair pouch…♥
next to the bronze panel with the floor buttons the
little hair pouch…♥
was fastened with a tiny yarn loop like a tunic (but smaller)
I opened the
little hair pouch…♥
and found

- a number of 50 CFA franc coins
- a few euro cents
- an Australian dollar
- a Byzantine gold *nomisma* in the effigy of
  emperor **CONSTANTINE IX MONOMACHUS**
  (probably left here by another Byzantine tourist)

and that's all I'm going to say for now, thanks for listening.

2

Now that we understand more about the relationship between great men and elevators, let us return to the life of my glorious father the Emperor, and see if we can continue dodging the question of supernatural portals by reading more poetry about coins.

But first a bit of history: it so happened that on October 10, 1081, the Normans landed at Dyrrachium on the Western coast of our Empire, having crossed the Adriatic sea with a hundred and fifty ships carrying fifteen thousand men with horses and catapults, led in their sanguinary folly by a certain Bohemond of Antioch. These are the events I will now endeavor to recount.

Bohemond, you see, was very tall, with long blond hair and a broad chest. I have often imagined what it must have been like to be his horse, carrying his warm, firm body into battle: his legs astride, his long, hard, shiny sword drawn out, his hips nudging with each step, slow and gentle at first, then faster and faster as he galloped to victory, hair, skin, leather, and metal caressing and flexing, his limbs tensing and sweating as he thrust himself into battle and screamed in triumph.

In any case, the battle of Dyrrachium lasted eight years. It followed the ancient rules of the chronodrome™. Limestone is heated over a great fire and mixed with water until quicklime is obtained. Then a circular clock face is drawn on the ground with a solution of quicklime and water, two stadia in diameter, and that perimeter becomes an inviolable portal space until someone dies. A sharp conical spike, two feet tall and made of cast iron, is placed in the exact center, with the tip up — which makes me think of Bohemond again for some reason.

A clock hand, made of a single trunk of beech beveled to a point at one end, flattened into a square tray at the other end, is brought in, and hinged on the spike in the center. At this point I'd like to offer another little poem about coins:

the square end of the clock hand

is LADEN with SACKS of

BRONZE COINS*

(*so the clock balances on the spike)

despite being much longer on one end

Two contestants, one for each warring side, challenge one another on the chronodrome™.

Time is set in motion by firing a gun into the air.

```
instructions:
the gun is fired → by an adolescent virgin girl
if none are available → by a certified accountant
if none are available → by a boy < 5 years old
if none are available → by a dog or a wild animal.
```

Once the gun is fired, the clock hand begins to spin and time elapses for all within the perimeter of the chronodrome™. The competitors have to run at the same speed as the clock hand. If they run faster, they become younger and younger until they are unborn, at which point they lose because they don't exist yet.

The opposite situation is more common: if the competitors run slower than the clock hand, time passes them by and they age until they're too tired to catch up. When a gray-haired competitor slows down and runs out of breath, his fate is sealed. He gets even older and more tired and never recovers. Soon he can barely move and dies of old age and turns to dust on the clock face.

The Normans entered Bohemond's father as their champion: Duke Robert Guiscard, a ruthless adventurer and miscreant. Our side entered General George Paleologos, a faithful soldier of Christ and loyal servant of his emperor.

They ran for eight years, seven months, eleven days, six hours, and six minutes, both armies watching silently from the sides, biting their tongue, holding their breath, stroking their beards, and eating peanuts out of big sacks. Both contestants died of old age, Duke Guiscard at the age of one hundred and seven, General Paleologos at the age of one hundred and twelve. Neither was buried as a Christian — the dust of their remains still lies on the ground where it fell. To this day, the battlefield is still littered with the peanut shells left by the belligerents.

And so the battle was inconclusive. On the Norman side the heinous, hunky Bohemond took the helm of the barbarian army after the death of Guiscard. On our side, my father, Emperor Alexios, assumed command of the defenders of our faith and civilization.

I wish I had been there, fighting at my father's side. With power tools I could have done so much for my country. Just give me a staple gun, I would have stapled our enemies' hair onto their beds so they couldn't get up.

But my lot was to have been born after the battle of Dyrrachium. So instead, with God's help, I will staple my father's glory onto the pages of history and roam the world in search of suitably masc metaphors of penetration.

3

Back in Yamoussoukro, in the shade of a corrugated tin awning, a cheerful young lady named Chantal was grilling rats. Chantal had big rats, small rats, medium rats, all grilled to perfection. She picked up two of them by the tail and held them in front of my camera, grinning for Byzantine social media.

"Rats!" she said as I filmed.

"So these are rats?"

"Yes, rats!" she announced triumphantly, as if to assure the Imperial Council that her victory over the heretics was complete.

I ordered fish and marveled at the dual-diarrhea design: freshly washed lettuce on the right, which works bacteriologically by relying on fecal pathogens naturally present in Yamoussoukro's tap water to overwhelm gut flora, and hot peppers on the left, which work chemically by stimulating cellular ion channel receptors and inducing intestinal convulsions. This was modular redundancy — very good engineering.

I hovered around the grill contentedly, watching my tilapia sear in the company of big rats and small rats. I breathed aromatic coal fumes and the fragrance of browned rat. I felt relieved.

Chantal dipped a wet rag in a bucket of fecally contaminated tap water and spread it over the cutting surfaces of her outdoor kitchen, then over my table and my neighbor's table, until all was clean. She also dipped a plate and, at my request, silverware, into the bucket and brought them to me.

"So what do you want?" she asked with a smile as she brought my food.

"Uhm, like, for dessert?" I asked.

"No in general. In life. Why are you dressed like this?"

"Oh. Uh. Well. I suppose I am a bit overdressed for the weather? Yamoussoukro is really quite hot, isn't it," I mumbled.

Chantal put my plate down, shrugged, and walked back to her rats.

The power briefly went off, then came back on, turning on two sets of animated musical Christmas lights that played favorite holiday tunes half a second apart. I waited for the sequence of holiday tunes to run its course like a bout of diarrhea, but it didn't. By the seventh tune I got up and ripped the power supply out of the wall socket.

All was still, dirty, and serene again: the rats, the coals, the freshly cleaned tables, the fecal water, the harsh bright day ebbing softly in the rich diesel haze of a cool evening.

I ate with joy and appetite.

4

The battle of Dyrrachium was a key moment of my father's rise to imperial power, but as a military event it was inconclusive. The Norman invaders didn't just leave. They pitched their camp outside the city, and assembled a great number of macho knights and soldiers with thick necks and big arms and muscular thighs and fierce blond beards. Their sturdy hands held gleaming lances, hard and sharp, ready to penetrate the flesh of their enemies — like stout straws thrusting into a hapless milkshake.

At sea, their enormous fleet, composed of every kind of ship, nearly surrounded the city, for Dyrrachium was built on a peninsula. My father Alexios, a brave man who had fought and won thousands of battles in barbarian lands, was unfazed. He began fortifying the city, building bulwarks, placing catapults on the walls, putting watchmen all along, and installing pomegranate dispensers at strategic locations in case he ever had a craving.

Meanwhile the Normans arrayed siege catapults outside the walls of Dyrrachium and built an enormous tower, even taller than the city walls. More ships arrived, more Normans disembarked and pitched more tents around the city.

I have often imagined what these tents must have been like, especially at night, with dozens of butch blond bearded young men sleeping in close quarters, probably naked, eating and showering together, their shiny, hard, sharp swords touching tips, shafts, and hilts. It must have smelled of man, armpit sweat, foot sweat, crotch sweat, and hormones. I wonder if friendships formed and bodies brushed and communed, or if these men were nothing more than brutal, barbarian heretics, driven by greed and hatred.

In any case, my father did not fear the savages. At dawn he made pancakes for everyone, in a big cast iron cauldron, with blueberries and maple syrup.

His men loved him, for they loved pancakes, and partaking of this generous breakfast was a holy moment of communion. The townsfolk also took heart, for the high sugar content of maple syrup released endorphins in their blood that helped them see that relief and victory was at hand. Then the Normans attacked and killed nearly everyone, despite the pancakes. They pushed the lustrous steel head of their weapons in and out of Greek flesh until it was wet, and the flesh spread open and gushed, and their endorphin-rich blood watered the ground of this happy city.

My father Alexios was still unconcerned. He sent an embassy to the Venetians with eighteen sacks of gold to bribe them into battle, promising them eighteen more — as well as every young woman in the city and half his reserves of peanuts — if they sailed to Dyrrachium with their navy and helped our side repel the Normans. Upon hearing this, the Venetians agreed and sailed for Dyrrachium. When night fell, they tied their largest ships together with ropes and built wooden towers on them. Then they cut thick beams into huge bludgeons studded with sharp iron nails and hoisted them to the top of their masts.

At dawn Bohemond came to them demanding they surrender, but instead the Venetians made fun of his blond beard, saying he looked like Santa Claus and Johannes Brahms. Bohemond was infuriated, because he hated Brahms and generally all romantic-era music, so he attacked them with his entire fleet. However, the Venetians hurled down their nail-studded bludgeons at the Norman vessels and, blasting the worst of Brahms string quartets from makeshift nautical loudspeakers, they gashed a huge hole into Bohemond's ship, and it began to sink. Some Normans jumped into the water and drowned, others kept fighting and were killed, sometimes on cue with specific tonal cadences. Bohemond leapt onto another ship and saved himself, but the Normans as a whole were routed and dispersed in the attack.

Afterwards the Venetians returned to their ships and my father Alexios, in his bravery, gave them the remaining eighteen sacks of gold he had promised as a bribe, as well as all the young women of Dyrrachium and a whole lot of peanuts. Festivities were held to celebrate the fact that these young women would be raped by our allies rather than our enemies, and panegyric poems were read aloud to wish them godspeed in that venture. The ground of the city was littered with peanut shells for months afterward.

My father then returned to Constantinople, where he was hailed as a hero for saving himself and a few other men, and for the divine inspiration that had prompted the pancake stratagem. Bohemond retreated to his tent, masturbated, and fell asleep stroking his beard.

II

Imperial Road Trip Apocalypse

1

After I had visited Yamoussoukro's famous basilica, eaten grilled tilapia, and slept, I flew to Mali (on Yamoussoukro Airlines, twice a week, it was last minute but I got a very good deal).

Now in Mali there a great old city called Ségou, and in its center is the illustrious Ségou market, a huge cylindrical tower made of piled-up cinder blocks. The floors are bare cement and the windows have no glass. It has twenty-six circular floors, each of them of sufficient diameter to accommodate hundreds of stalls. The entire building is a supernatural portal into the political architecture of the cosmos, and it can only be described in poetic form. And that's the next monument I needed to research after Yamoussoukro and its basilica.

The Ségou market is a basilica of a different kind. It was not made by one big macho man with mass murder and mass theft in the service of his own power, like the one in Yamoussoukro, but by many little macho men, who go daily about the business of minor murder and minor theft in the exercise of minor power. Such a place is called a *market*. And that brand of habitual violence is called *the market economy*.

Please join me now (poetry only) into the Ségou market.

Floor 1.

The first floor of the market is the realm of Peul herders and their flocks. It is divided into four quadrants, for cows of the four elemental colors:

black
white
ochre
&
yellow

those quadrants are oriented

North

West   East

South

and tended by the herders of the

air
water
earth
&
fire

clans, respectively

Above each stall is a leather effigy of Ndurbeele

Ndurbeele is the original hermaphrodite bovine of Peul
mythology
> the archetypal primal ancestor of all herds
> the gender-nonbinary bovine parent of all cows and
> bulls
> the vital source of all milk and sperm

Do you see why I need to mention Ndurbeele now?
> we have a masc emperor in Constantinople — dad
> I'm writing his biography
> the Peul have a nonbinary bovine founder character

BUT

surely Ndurbeele is hairier than dad

bc Ndurbeele is literally an animal

we've already encountered this problem with the hair elevator

I feel like so many problems are related to hair

Between the four quadrants are

    three rows of thornbush hedges
    three quiet little circular clearings
                    each containing
    lawnmower spare parts

One of the clearings also has

    a used condom
    a clump of partially shredded plastic bags
                  (black, blue, and white)
    the top half of an oil filter from a 1997 Toyota Corolla.

People don't go into these clearings, they are sacred spaces.

Floor 2.

The second floor has milk stored in large blue plastic containers with stickers that say:

对水生生物毒性非常大 - `very toxicity to aquatic life`

2

After only two floors I needed to go to the bathroom — sorry. Byzantine princesses do use the bathroom, too, even if imperial chronicles don't report it.

I ambled toward the public toilet facility across the street from the market. I fumbled into my pockets looking for a few coins, and wondered if I could get away with paying with a Byzantine *nomisma* in the effigy of my own father. If not, I'd make change at the automatic pomegranate dispenser. Daddy would be glad to know his face got to tumble into a pomegranate machine in a faraway land in Africa.

You don't need to come with me for this episode — actually why don't you stay here and watch this scene from a distance: people constantly streaming in and out of the building, with children running after each customer to collect the fee.

Above the left-hand side entrance a hand-painted sign: MEN.
On the right-hand side: WOMEN.

I tentatively inched toward the middle, as if a door was going to open there for me. I walked slowly and carefully, treading silently, avoiding eye contact, as if approaching a herd of grazing water buffalo.

One step at a time.
One more step.
One more little step.
One more.

Suddenly the whole herd looked up. There was a predatory Byzantine princess on the prowl, in a flowing yellow skirt.

Everyone stopped walking, talking, and counting money, and looked at me, not straight, but

sideways
> *over their shoulder*
>> *at an angle*
>>> *diagonally*
>>>> *laterally*
>>>>> *obliquely*
>>>>>> as if by some fluke

nobody's head had been pointing in my direction just a second
earlier

,

then

hundreds of men QUIZZED me with their gaze:

♥Are you going to violate the sacred masculine space of our segregated toilet?♥

are you going to subject us   to the indignity of your presence

EVEN IN THE PRIVACY OF OUR COLLECTIVE EXCRETION?

MUST WE

DEFEND OUR TERRITORY

AND

TAKE UP ARMS

THE DIARY OF ANNA COMNENA

Hundreds of women folded their arms across their chest, pointed their chins, pursed their lips, and stared at me:

> "This is a reserved space"

their folded elbows said, sharp as horns. \ /. \ /. \ /. \ /.

I retreated like an intimidated child. I wondered if someone would step up from behind and touch me like Jesus touched the leper in the Gospels, and say: "I love you stranger. If you belong neither on the left nor on the right, then you can use the restroom in the back of my shop."

But nobody did.

I gave up on **my subversive project** and turned around.

At that instant someone released the pause button for the public restroom in Ségou, and all the characters at once reverted to their

walking
    talking   shouting
        counting   money   123456789
    jostling   hustling
  bustling

The soundtrack returned. A Peugeot pick-up truck drove by, blaring election propaganda from a tired gritty loudspeaker. The predator was gone.

I hailed a taxi, a 1997 Toyota Corolla of the kind usually found in sacred liminal spaces, this particular one with one blue door and "Allahou Akbarou" handpainted on the trunk.

"Good afternoon young man! Where are you going?" said the driver cheerfully.

I bit my lip and said nothing for a while out of distraction.

"I'll walk, it's OK," I said finally. The taxi sped away.

I hailed another taxi, a 2003 Renault Mégane with thick beige synthetic fur on the dashboard and every seat, and "Rambo Terminator Man" hand-painted on the trunk.

"Good afternoon young man! Where are you going?" said the driver cheerfully.

I took a deep breath and said nothing.

"I'll walk, it's OK," I said finally. The taxi sped away.

I hailed another taxi, a 1993 Mercedes C-class with one headlight and a gasoline canister on the passenger seat connected to the dashboard by a plastic tube, and "N'oublie pas ta maman" hand-painted on the trunk.

"Good afternoon young man! Where are you going?" said the driver cheerfully.

I clenched my teeth and said nothing.

"I'll walk, it's OK," I said finally. The taxi sped away.

I walked to my hotel. I walked fast and used the restroom there.

3

Darkness is freedom. Darkness is safety. I am invisible and everyone is blind.

When night fell I walked back out of my hotel into the dusty alleys of Ségou, a thin embroidered veil over my head, a chiseled brass bracelet around each of my wrists, octagonal plastic beads strung by an elastic band around my neck, the billows of my skirt following me like a friendly, wispy shadow.

I walked away from the light and in the darkest direction possible, into the blackest, loneliest, and narrowest alleys, where safety and peace awaited me. I walked for a while until I was completely wrapped in darkness and I could see nothing at all, feeling safe and free in the blind urban night, occasionally surrounded by anonymous friends brushing against me and conversations between shadows. Then

finally on a street corner I saw three teenagers
sitting on the sidewalk with a makeshift
food stand and a little flashlight.
On the stand were a few cuts
of meat and two little
pieces of fish
cucumbers
peppers
salt

(in a blue plastic bag)
a plastic plate, water, and a machete.

      I bowed to them /////// — for surely they were angels
      I sat next to them on the sidewalk
      I gestured at the fish \ /. \ /. \ /. \ /.
      I gave them a few coins

food appeared.

I ate silently in the dark
sitting on the sidewalk
my skirt in the gutter
my left hand holding up my plate
my right hand cupped into a ladle
ferrying the feast into my mouth.

Then someone touched my shoulder from behind and offered
me a little plastic stool.

I gratefully accepted
both the stool
and the touch
Jesus had not forgotten his leper after all.

For an instant I glimpsed what it would be like to partake of a
divine feast seated on a celestial armchair at the heavenly table.
It would be this meal of fish flakes, this little plastic stool, and
three angels on a dark sidewalk in paradise, all transfigured by
that godly touch on my shoulder.

I let my greasy right hand dangle above the plastic plate
                                                    for a moment

I breathed the healing darkness of this street corner deep into
my body
and
pronounced my meal:

a Thanksgiving supper.

4

I have more to say about the market in Ségou, but I was a bit distracted by the whole bathroom episode.

A savory detail, though: carrying a gold nomisma in the effigy of my own father was not sufficient to get me access to a bathroom. Anyway, I cannot let myself be sidetracked by these bathroom trifles, which would be unbecoming of a purple-born Byzantine princess and of the propriety required by my rank. I remain as committed as ever to my mission: composing an imperial biography worthy of my father's glory.

BUT

Every Imperial Biography Involves a Long Road Trip

And this one is no exception. It will take us from Ségou to Conakry, the capital of Guinea, which is known for excellent seafood as well as angels wielding power tools. Perhaps I'll feel more collected in a moving vehicle.

On the road from Ségou to Conakry, I sat in a 1984 Peugeot station wagon next to a young man from Nzérékoré named Moïse, who later turned out to be an angel with connections in the world of power tools.

Moïse had tried his luck in Dakar as a teenager, made some money, and spent it on alcohol and parties. Then he had tried his luck again in Mali and made enough money to save for a bus trip. And now he was twenty years old and he was going to try his luck in Conakry. Angels have careers, too.

"Why Conakry?" I asked as we pulled out of Ségou's bus terminal.

"I've already tried everywhere else," Moïse said. "Nzérékoré, Dakar, Tambacounda, Ségou — everywhere. I've literally been everywhere. So now I want to try Conakry, you see?"

"I see. So you didn't like Nzérékoré?" I asked.

"Ehh, what are you talking about, princess, Nzérékoré is the best!"

"But?"

"But I don't want to be in my hometown all my life. I'm already twenty, my clock is ticking. I want to see the world," Moïse said.

"Of course," I acquiesced. "I'm glad you still like your hometown. It sounds like a lovely place."

"Yes, Guinée-Forestière is the best part of Guinea. It's like paradise. We have bananas, cassava, and bushmeat. The forest is rich, everything grows there."

"How wonderful," I said.

"My favorite meat is cow," Moïse added. "When I have a chance, I will eat cow meat. Have you tried cow meat, princess?"

"I don't eat meat, but I'm sure it's delicious," I said.

"Princess, if you save some money, you can buy cow meat. I think when you try it you will like cow meat too much!" he said.

"Well thank you for that recommendation, I'll make sure to keep that in mind," I said.

As we left Ségou and merged onto the open road, our vehicle found a humming stride and the landscape began to unfurl at cruising speed for about

like

25 seconds before we hit this massive

(ow)   po^{thole}

like massive giant pothole like   M—A—S—S—I—V—E
                          cosmic

RUT

      I swear we hadn't been out of Ségou for
               "even a minute"

My phone fell out of my handbag into a sack of Moon Boké brand peanuts. The cardboard effigy of Nelson Mandela hanging from the rear view mirror swung hard into the windshield, bruising the late stateman's shoulder. My backpack tipped over, spilling most of my underwear onto a live chicken, except for one piece (that had been worn for just a few minutes) onto a lady's face, which she soon swatted down onto the chicken. Everyone found themselves sitting halfway up their neighbor's thigh for just a brief second. There was much rumbling, grumbling, dust, and apocalypse.

Then everything and everyone was put back into its rightful place and we proceeded smoothly down the open road, as the vehicle found a humming stride and the landscape began to unfurl at cruising speed again for about

like

2 minutes I swear before we got stopped

by an army checkpoint *!!!*

A young soldier

papers
papers
bribe
greetings
wave, (fake) smile, salutations

back on our way.

"Tell me about Dakar. Was it nice living there?" I asked calmly and cheerfully, summoning the "this apocalypse is OK" tone that experienced transgender Byzantine princesses have in their repertoire.

"Ah! Was Dakar nice! Dakar, princess! Dakar is Dakar! Have you ever been to Dakar?" Moïse asked.

"Yes, several times," I said.

"Dakar is a nonstop party!" he said.

"That wasn't quite my experience, but I still enjoyed my visit," I said.

"You don't like to party?" he asked.

I thought about it for a moment, looking at my dust-coated arms as if the answer was carved in my arm hair. "Well I'm a bit older than you. And I'm a Byzantine princess. So perhaps I don't party quite as much?"

"Come on princess, how are those things connected in your mind? Princesses don't party? Or they stop partying after a certain age?" he asked.

"Oh… well, I suppose I carry with my person a certain… a certain expectation of propriety?" I said.

"Ehh, who taught you that word?" Moïse asked.

"Well, I mean…"

"Actually, princess, what do you want?" he asked before I could answer the previous question.

The first word that came to my mind was "oof" but instead I remained silent with my mouth half-open. Then we hit a

M~A~S~S~I~V~E cosmic

RUT

underwear
→ chicken

phone → peanuts,
etc

I noticed a faint salty taste in my mouth and realized I had bit my tongue as the

relentless ruts of the Malian road had

punished my *certain expectation of propriety*

by **SLAMMING** my
half-gaping
silent
"oof"
</shut>

My conversation with Moïse was obviously shaped like the road to Conakry. There was no smooth build-up — minutes into the journey I was already being stirred and jolted and searched and questioned. One moment I thought I was comfortably seated and my bag was neatly packed, the next moment a rut shook me off my seat and spilled my underwear all over the floor.

And if I tried to get away with a silent "oof"

t::here would be bloo::d

"I'm not sure why I don't party actually. It's a good question," I said, running out of credible propriety vibe.

Moïse frowned.

"Maybe I just don't like to party?" I offered while tidying up my spilled underwear.

"Nah… princess. I don't believe you," Moïse said. He continued: "I think you just didn't find the right parties. Did you try a party with a Byzantine princess DJ?"

"Well." I tried to say something witty, but I felt stiff. I consciously kept my mouth closed and my tongue out of reach of the Malian road.

I really wanted this conversation to end — it was lurching in uncomfortable fits and starts and going in an awkward direction — but I also wanted it to continue, and probably for the same reason.

"Well I love the idea but I'm not sure they have that in Dakar," I said finally.

"Ha! Haaaa! They have *everything* in Dakar! Did you even look?" Moïse exclaimed.

"I guess not. I didn't look for Byzantine DJ parties in Dakar," I conceded.

"See? You gotta dig into the reality instead of making assumptions."

"Fair. I guess I also don't drink, so… parties without alcohol?" I said, hoping Moïse would see through my bad faith and dismiss my feeble objection.

"Ahaaaaa you're gonna party with the Muslim Brotherhood!" he said instead.

"Well. I might? Do they party much?" I asked, tired of my own courtliness.

"Hehe actually I don't really know what they do. But they don't drink."

We paused. It felt like we had missed a turn. Moïse buried his nose in his phone for a while. I nodded off. I probably slept for about an hour. I had hoped for this conversation to be apocalypse-worthy. The stuff of novels. But instead we had missed that turn and now the road trip had turned kinda pedestrian.

When I woke up the landscape hadn't changed. It was still flattish and predominantly ochre and green, with a mixture of dusty banana trees, nondescript bush, an occasional moped, an occasional fruit stand, occasional birds — like a rough draft of a video game. A sloppy copy-and-paste job awaiting to be fleshed out.

We hit another rut — underwear↩→chicken↩→Moon Boké brand peanuts, etc.

Then Moïse fleshed it out, swinging like a cardboard Mandela off a rear view mirror:

"So princess, your turn to tell me about Dakar now. What is it like for you in Dakar actually? How is it on the street when you walk around like this?" he asked.

This time I gave up on "oof" and answered outright: "Dakar is tricky for me. If I walk down the street, everyone stares at me and makes fun of me," I said.

"Yeah."

"I mean — everyone. Thousands of people stare at me."

"Yeah."

"If I walk into a shop, everyone giggles," I added.

"Yeah."

"If I walk into a market, everyone starts to whisper."

"Yeah."

"Or they point at me and call me names."

"Yeah I see," he said.

We paused again.

I didn't want to miss the next turn. I continued: "Maybe they've never seen anybody like me?"

"Ohhh, come on, princess. Of course they have. There are lots of people like you."

"Where?" I asked.

"Everywhere. But they're scared, they hide. They stay inside." Moïse said.

"So how do you know they're everywhere?" I asked.

"Because I know them. There are people like you in Dakar. And in Conakry also. In all the big cities. You just have to know the right neighborhoods. You would have to know the right bar at the right time," Moïse said.

"But not on the street?" I asked.

"Come on princess, this is Africa. Not everything is public. If you're going to get along in Africa, you need to understand what's public and what's private. Some things we do only in private, and we don't talk about them." Moïse said.

This Is Africa. Not Everything Is Public.

"If you do them in public you're gonna get yourself in trouble," Moïse continued.

"Well, I seem to have achieved that." I said.

"Ehh."

"So what else is not done in public?" I asked.

"Didn't I just tell you we don't talk about that?" Moïse answered.

"I think you actually do want to talk about it," I said. "Right now you're hoping I'm going to insist hard so you can finally bring it up."

"How do you know?" Moïse asked.

"Because you would only tell a foreign tourist in a moving vehicle, and this is your chance. And otherwise you wouldn't have brought it up yourself."

Moïse pinched his lips, squinted, and wrinkled his nose. Now I had also embraced the brutal road to Conakry. There would be no slow build-up and no silent "oof" and no Byzantine propriety. We were going to do some questioning, some shaking, and some jolting.

there would be ruts

LET. UNDERWEAR. FLY.

"You're curious about many things, princess. Don't you just want to visit Africa and see the sights?" Moïse asked, now eager for me to brush aside his bad faith.

Then we didn't hit a rut, but instead it rained for twenty seconds and suddenly the windshield was clean.

Moïse and I realized simultaneously that we each had things to say, perhaps more to ourselves than to each other, and were not going to say them unless the other prodded and breached the weak barricades of our bad faith.

And God in his grace had locked both of us for hours next to a providential stranger — not just any stranger, but one so alien to our home universes, so stripped of any commonality besides the existential bond of the present moment, that each of us held up for the other the divine clarity of mirrored humanity.

5

I had a new vision of the Apocalypse. It was the road to Cona-kry—a slow, relentless Revelation, full of brutal ruts sending my underwear flying every which way across the car, leaving nothing in order, no matter how neatly packed, and this rusty old Peugeot inexorably filling up with God's presence like a drip fills a tin jug.

"Look, Moïse, I don't know if I'm being curious." I said. "Sure, I'm curious because I'm a historian and I like to know how things work. But I'm also a trans white outsider here, so I can never be a neutral observer. My sheer presence causes a chemical reaction wherever I go. As if there was something quietly dissolved or suspended in the air, and I cause it to precipitate and become visible."

"So what is it that becomes visible?" Moïse asked.

"When I talk to people in private," I said, "in a shop, in a taxi, in their home…"

"They open up?" he asked, completing my sentence.

"Well, in more ways than one. They tell me about their sexual fantasies, but they also try to act them out on me. They tell me about corruption, prostitution, emigration. They tell me their dark secrets because I'm a fictional character to them. They know I will disappear with their secret. There are no conse-quences," I said.

"So you already know what I was going to say," Moïse said.

"Maybe? Everyone has something different to say. I think you still have to name it. I'm a historian, not a diviner." I said.

"People don't talk about gender and sexuality in public in Af-rica," Moïse answered without any pause, as if that thought had been complete for a while in his mind but not cued to take the stage until I summoned it. "I think you already know that," he added. "And they don't display it if it's… different."

"Alright. Yes, I already knew that. But what else?" I asked.

"You mean what else is secret?" he asked, rhetorically, waiting for me to push a little harder, or for a second shower to clear the windshield again.

"People don't talk about corruption," I said. "Or prostitution. Or emigration. Those are shameful."

"So you've answered your own question," Moïse retorted.

"No I haven't. Shameful is not the same as secret. We're talking about things that are secret." I said.

He looked out the window, almost bit his nails, but then didn't. Then he continued more softly: "ok so we don't talk about witchcraft in public. People do it. Everyone does it. Every person you see in this car does it. But nobody talks about it."

"Witchcraft! I was waiting for you to say something like that," I said.

"Ehh. That's anticlimactic… I thought I was coming at you with a big revelation haha," he laughed. "So how did you know?" he asked.

"Because when people specifically avoid a topic, they end up carving out a hollow space shaped exactly like that object. Our Byzantine authors don't talk about magic either. They think about it, they might even do it, but they don't say so. They dance around the topic. After a while, if you follow the dance, you can see the shape of the forbidden area," I said.

"Yeah maybe. So gender and sexuality are the same as witchcraft. You follow the dance and you can see the shape of the forbidden area," Moïse said.

"And in the middle of that forbidden area is a supernatural portal to a different order of the universe," I said, "where rules are different and power is distributed differently. And that's why we don't go there. But that's also why we sometimes do."

We both paused for a while.

Moïse wasn't going to miss the next turn. He continued: "Look, people laugh at you because you make them very nervous. You're not supposed to be walking around Dakar like this. It's like you're spilling everyone's secret. It's not because they've never seen a trans person. On the contrary, it's because you're like the trans cousin they have locked up at home and that nobody talks about. And that cousin shouldn't be walking around in front of everyone. It's like you're giving everyone the keys to the forbidden area."

"I know. That's what it feels like," I said.

"And you're white," Moïse pointed out, not missing that turn either. "So you're not like their hidden cousin, because they actually can't just tell you to be quiet and stay home. Because you have money, and they need to eat. You have power. Whether you like it or not. The power is in your skin color. You can't take it out."

"And because I'm foreign, they can't read my motivations. They don't know if I'm being provocative or oblivious," I added. "Maybe I just came to Africa for the beach and the wild animals? Maybe I just have no idea and I'm just here for the Instagram moments? They can't read me."

"Ehh…yeah, the beach and wild animals of Ségou, lol… Actually I don't even understand what you were doing there. What's in Ségou for a Byzantine princess? Why would anyone go to Ségou… Actually why are you in Africa in the first place? Why are you on the road to Conakry with me? You haven't even told me," Moïse said.

"Well there's a whole story," I said.

"And does it have to do with you being trans?" Moïse asked before I could say more.

"Well…," I started again.

"And does it have to do with witchcraft?" he asked, interrupting me again.

"I'm trying to figure that one out. I'm scared to say yes or no," I said.

"Then I think you've said enough," Moïse said.

"But what about you Moïse? You're twenty years old, why did you leave Nzérékoré if it's so nice there? And why did you leave Dakar if it was so much fun? Why are *you* on the road to Conakry with me?" I asked.

"You know how to ask tricky questions, princess," he said.

"Does *your* story have to do with witchcraft? Do you notice you asked me that question first? Nobody has ever asked me that question in my entire life, it's not an innocent question," I pointed out.

"We both know how to ask tricky questions, princess," Moïse answered.

"Then I think you've also said enough," I said.

Moïse tilted his head back as if he was going to rest it on the pillow of our nascent, fragile, mutual epiphany. Then he looked straight ahead again and added: "You know, old people — they probably go do *wudu* and wash themselves ritually after they see you. And young people — they don't understand why you're not scared."

"I *am* scared," I said.

"OK, then they don't understand why you're not hiding," Moïse corrected.

"Because I'm not ashamed, just scared," I said.

"Yeah. Well. Don't be ashamed. God made you. God made all of us," Moïse said with a curious assurance.

"I think you're also scared but not hiding, Moïse," I said. "God made all of us."

I looked out the window and breathed in some red road dust as if it was incense. God had made me, and also Moïse. And now he had put us next to each other in a rusty old Peugeot to remind each other.

I tried to sleep again but the road got too pixelated. At that resolution everything was square. The wheels were square, the bananas were square, the potholes were square. The car moved in a series of low-resolution perpendicular jolts until my spine was square. All my bones were downgraded to their low-res version until my whole body was just a few bytes. My mind stopped spinning to preserve the contents of memory.

III

Fluid States

Fluid States

1

I'm not ready to talk more about witchcraft right now, but for the moment I'd like to tell you how the market in Ségou relates to yoghurt and gender.

If you also need to go to the bathroom and can do so safely where you are, you can use the rest of this page to take a little break.

then

when you're ready, turn to the next page.

Floor 3.

The third floor of the market in Ségou is where the yoghurt is made. Yoghurt is not quite fluid. It is made with a fluid, but then it gels as it ferments.

- It is left to ferment here until it turns solid.
  Then it is stirred until it turns liquid again.
  Then left to set until it turns solid again.
- Then stirred again.

  Then left to set again.

And so on indefinitely.

Repeat — it's a cosmic process that is constantly done and undone.

Yoghurt is a non-Newtonian fluid whose visco-elastic properties change under shearing stress. There is a special spiritual symbolism to that category of substance:

> yoghurt
> peanut butter
> ketchup
> hair gel

Those substances are the spirit fluids of specific Peul clans:

> air
> water
> earth
> and fire
> (respectively)

The viscosity of those fluids increases under stress: they become liquid when stirred, but gel again if left undisturbed for…

> (……………………………………
> …………………………………..)
> (……………………………………………
> …………………….*a certain amount of time*………………
> ………………………………..)
> (…………..

But that gelling time is   **++ FIXED ++**

it is actually a specific delay for yoghurt, and another for hair gel, etc. Gelling time is an immutable physical property of each substance.

> In olden times, Peul herders considered the reversibility of these substances
> > from fluid to → solid
> and back again ←

to be an allegory of the cyclical nature of Creation, a reminder of the vanity of earthly endeavors and the need to submit to divine forces.

Long ago, according to oral tradition, there was even a fifth elemental clan:

> the plasma clan.

Ancestors from that plasma clan had above-average spiritual powers,
not quite super-human,
but not quite human either.

Their spirit non-Newtonian fluid was

mayonnaise
whose gelling time
back to a highly viscous
near-solid state
after being liquefied
by stirring is
almost instant
It is however:

not quite instant.

Floors 4–7.

If these floors exist at all (not sure), they harbor the non-Newtonian gender substance that is the spirit fluid of the nonbinary bovine of Peul mythology. It has a property called

RHEOPEXY

which is the opposite behavior of yoghurt and ketchup:

it SOLIDIFIES under stress

imagine!

but as long   as it is left   [alone]

it remains *fluid…*♥
and flows *freely…*♥

yay

watery sand has this property:

it is solid and dry when _{stepped on} and *crushed…*♥

otherwise it is malleable
even liquid

I wonder if my own blood is made of watery sand??
for surely my spirit fluid is non——————— Newtonian
and my gender has the hallmarks of rheopexy.

2

At the border crossing into Guinea everyone had to leave the vehicle.

"What is your name?" asked a guard.

"Anna Comnena" I said.

"Where are you from?"

"Constantinople"

"What is your profession?"

"Historian and chronicler."

"What is your father's profession?"

"Byzantine Emperor."

The guard dutifully wrote everything down with a ballpoint pen in a ruled elementary school notebook, just beneath the details of Candice Wong, yoga instructor from Brisbane, Australia, and Abbas ibn Rashid al-Andalusi, salt trader from Granada.

"What is your date of birth?" he added.

"December 1st, 1083," I said.

He looked up from behind his desk.

"So you didn't actually witness the battle of Dyrrachium first hand? You weren't even born," he said.

"True. But I grew up hearing all about it. I mean — anyone is welcome to write about it, but so far I'm the best source — I think."

"So what do you want?" he asked finally.

"Like... in general?"

"Why are you in Guinea dressed like this?"

"Oh... uhm... I'm here to write an imperial biography," I said.

He shrugged and went on to question the next traveler.

I walked to the next office and handed my passport. I was led into a little windowless room in the back where two armed uniformed men searched my bag. They poked around my socks and underwear and found a chicken feather and a few peanut shells, as well as my lipstick and my nail polish.

"And what is this, **SIR**?" they asked triumphantly, holding up the lipstick.
"Lipstick," I said.

"And why do you have it, **SIR**?"
"To put on my lips."
"And what is this now?" they asked, holding up my nail polish.
"Nail polish," I said.

"And why do you travel with nail polish, **SIR**?"
"To put on my nails," I said.

Both times they seemed disappointed at my answer, as if they had expected a tearful confession. They stood perplexed, my cosmetics in one hand, their guns in the other, like hungry leopards trained to pounce on a running gazelle, but disoriented that the gazelle is not running.

I gently collected my lipstick and nail polish out of their hands, calmly put them back in my backpack, zipped it up, and asked:

"Do you have any other questions for me?"

They stood between me and the door and responded:

"Do you have any gifts for us?"

"Yes, you have my blessings. Consider it your luck, for spiritual gifts are eternal and their value does not fade," I said, raising my right palm in front of my face in a gesture of blessing.

One guard clenched his lips in anger. The other one burst out laughing and opened the door, saying: "Get the fuck out of here already."

I collected my bag and walked out.

"You are brave," said Moïse as we met again outside.
"No, I am numb."
"But you are not scared of the guards?"

"I think my blood is made of watery sand," I said, "so I solidify under stress, and then I will liquefy again later. This is what happens when your fluid spirit is non-Newtonian. It's called rheopexy."

3

In all liminal spaces, there is a 1997 Toyota Corolla. I'm half-seriously thinking there must have been one at the battle of Dyrrachium, too.

After the border formalities, a man approached me with a stack of half-shredded, brownish bills and offered to change currency. I laid out my money on the hood of the nearest 1997 Toyota Corolla, we counted it together, and he gave me exact change against the windshield.

The money changer introduced himself as Seydou. I learned that he had a 16-year-old son called Lamine who likes computers and wants to become an engineer. I told him about my own struggles being the child of a Byzantine emperor.

He asked me if currency exchange worked differently in my country. I said that we only use coins, and that my father had replaced the old debased *nomisma* with a new, slightly concave *hyperpyron* gold coin in his effigy. Seydou said his own father had a fine herd of sheep up in the hills of the Fouta Djalon, but had never had any gold coins minted in his effigy. The effigy was not the point, I explained, you could still use coins in the effigy of previous emperors. Seydou was not convinced.

But I insisted: the point was their gold contents. *Nomismata* used to be 24 carat pure gold, but they had been gradually debased over the years and their gold contents reduced until they were essentially worthless pieces of tin. My father's genius had been to get rid of these useless *nomismata* and melt them into a new standard 20.5 carat gold *hyperpyron* coins.

What was brilliant and novel about his idea was to assign monetary value to a specific proportion, rather to the purity of a substance. It was the ratio of gold to silver in electrum coins that gave them their value, and the ratio of silver to copper in billon coins.

Mathematics could now transfigure impurity and turn in-between states into standards, and margins into center. Soon the world would abandon its essentialist fixation with things being either wholly one thing or wholly another and warm up to the value of fluid and nonbinary coins.

Purses would welcome not just
ELECTRUM and **BILLON**
but soon also:

	copper	lead	gold	silver	mercury	tin	antimony
HEPATIZON	X		X	X			
MOLYBDOCHALKOS	X	X					
BRASS			*(do you know that one?)*				
ORMOLU			X		X		
SHAKUDO	X		X				
SHIBUICHI	X			X			
PEWTER						X	X
TERNE		X				X	

and EVERY other alloy, and even perhaps
nonbinary alloys of metal with
wood~~~~~~~~~~~~~~~~yes
hair gel~~~~~~~~~~~~~~~yes
peanut butter~~~~~~~~~~~yes
plasma~~~~~~~~~~~~~~~~~yes

with Newtonian and non-Newtonian fluids living in peace with each other and even with

SOLIDS

(~~~~~~~~~~like, I don't hate them~~~~~~~~~~)

But NO — the world is STUBBORN and people are ESSENTIAL-ISTS:

  even my father's own private secretary, John Zonaras, misunderstood the coinage reform and went on record disparaging it because **HE COULD NOT CONCEIVE** of a **WORTHY COIN** being made of anything else than

PURE GOLD
or
PURE SILVER
or
PURE COPPER
or pure this and pure that
all
metals for medals™ — bc men just gotta win

Anyway what should I care about people like John Zonaras — he also thought chess playing was evil and throwing dice was a sin. Perhaps I should care less what people like that have to say about alloys, and not let such narrow-mindedness bother me. Argh.

"So what your father did was like stitch a 20,000 Guinean franc bill to a 5,000 CFA franc bill?" Seydou asked me, interrupting my private musings about the morality of alloys.

"Well…not exactly," I said.

"Actually, no, I see," he corrected. "It is like what my own father does up in the hills of the Fouta Djalon with his sheep. He breeds one kind with another, so they are stronger. Then the value of the sheep is higher when they are mixed between different kinds of sheep. And your father is doing this with coins because he doesn't have any sheep. Is that right?"

"I think that…might actually be right, yes," I said.

"But why concave?" Seydou asked.

"The coins?" I asked.

"Yes, not the sheep obviously. You said earlier the new *hyper-pyron* was slightly concave," he said.

"Ah… yes, we call that shape *scyphate* — I don't really know where that word comes from actually," I said.

"Yes, but I'm not asking what the shape is called in your dialect, I'm asking why concave? Why not flat coins?" Seydou explained.

"Well, to be honest I never quite understood what the point was, and why that was a better idea than minting plain flat disks," I said. "But surely my father had a good reason for preferring those. He usually has good ideas. That's why God made him Emperor."

I'm not sure why I said that to Seydou, but I felt dutiful and pious saying it.

Anyway Seydou asked me if money changers often became Byzantine Emperors, considering how much the job seemed to revolve around coinage. I said it wasn't a prerequisite. The job had many other facets such as waging war on heretics and selling local women to Venetian mercenaries and making pancakes with maple syrup.

In fact, we had only had one emperor who had been a money changer — Michael IV the Paphlagonian. He hadn't made such a positive impression, even in matters of coinage policy really.

Seydou seemed disappointed. I scoured my memory for another money-changing emperor but couldn't name one. We wished each other good luck and parted.

4

One midsummer evening, my father Alexios summoned me and my younger brother Bobby into his private office.

The Emperor's private office was on the first floor of the new Blachernae Palace, overlooking the gray waters of the Bosphorus. It was a big cubic room with a very tall ceiling. Nearly everything in it was cedar. The walls were cedar panels finished in a dark red veneer, with hunting scenes rendered in marquetry delineated with inlaid pewter showing centaurs and buffalo. The ceiling was a rich dark shade of varnished cedar studded with pearls of different sizes arranged in the shape of the constellations. The floor was a glossy polished cedar parquet adorned with an illustrated map of the Empire carved out in intarsia just beneath a layer of shellac wax. In the corner was a wall-mounted rotary telephone made of solid blond cedar, connected to the wall by a cedar cord. The unwieldy location and the outdated model betrayed the reluctant relationship of men of my father's age to technology.

In the middle of the room was a very long rectangular cedar table veneered with tortoiseshell, brass, and ivory, with eight feet shaped like lion claws resting on felt pads.

My father was dressed in a black velvet robe lined with gold, except for a loose gray sweater that read "I fought the battle of Dyrrachium and all I got was this lousy sweater" — his way of signaling that this was an informal meeting. He sat at the far end of the table. Bobby and I sat at the other end.

"My boys," said my father calmly. Bobby smiled and clasped his hands together.

A long pause followed.

My father pulled a lever and a little spring-loaded tray popped out of the table with a creaking noise, bearing a golden cup filled with pomegranate seeds and a single golden toothpick. He helped himself to a dozen pomegranate seeds, chewed them in silence, then pushed the tray back into the table.

It clicked.

"My boys," said my father again after a while. I felt a metallic taste in my mouth and realized I had been biting my tongue so hard it was bleeding.

He continued: "I wanted to speak to you both about our Empire, and the need for one of you to join me on the throne, and eventually to succeed me."

"You are the elder son," he said, looking at me lovingly. "But I think you need some time to find a wife. And to start a family. And perhaps to find yourself. Or perhaps you do not wish for the things that most men want, and an ecclesiastical career would suit you better?"

I said nothing. I felt like I was being petted with a cast iron glove running a steel rake through my scalp.

"You, Bobby," he continued, "are the younger one, and your two winsome children are still infants. But your beautiful wife will raise them to make the Empire proud. Perhaps it would be best for you to begin acquainting yourself with the affairs of the State, as I think it will be your calling to lead it one day."

I looked at the cedar floor and lost myself in the cedar seas and the cedar mountains of the imperial map. Then I looked at the walls, rubbed my nose and fought a centaur for a while. Bobby put his hand on my knee to stop me bouncing my leg.

I tried to say something but only blood and saliva dribbled out of my mouth.

"If you have no further questions, then you may both go," said my father after a while. Bobby got up, bowed, and left.

"Next week is the Feast of the Transfiguration," he added, addressing me as I was also preparing to leave. "Since you're usually so full of clever talk — except today, I notice — then you should deliver the sermon, and we will see if an ecclesiastical career is for you." I nodded silently, got up, bowed, and left.

5

On the Guinean side of the border I found Moïse sitting on a bench, eating peanuts from a Moon Boké sack. I sat next to him.

"Would you like some peanuts?" he asked.

"No, thank you." I said.

"You know, in Nzérékoré, where I'm from, everybody would accept you as you are," he said.

"Well, I should visit Nzérékoré some day," I said.

"Yes, you should," Moïse said, then added: "We can have cow meat."

"Tell me, Moïse, where will you stay when you arrive in Conakry?" I asked, changing the topic away from cow meat.

"I don't know yet. I think I have an uncle there. But don't worry about me, I'll find something. What about you?" he asked.

"I will sleep in a hotel," I said.

"Ehh, Byzantine people like hotels, don't they?" Moïse commented. "So how long will you stay in the hotel there?"

"I don't know, maybe a few days?"

"And then go back to your country?" he asked.

"No, I will keep traveling," I said.

"You don't want to go back to your country, do you?" Moïse asked.

I nodded sideways, looked down at the wooden bench we shared, and marveled at the clarity of mind of the young angel of Nzérékoré.

"Are you sure you don't want any peanuts?" Moïse asked.

"No thanks, I'm ok," I said.

"A lot of people don't want to go back home, you know," he continued, dropping peanut shells on the ground.

I stared at my feet and at the peanut shells and said nothing in silent agreement.

"Not just princesses. Everyone has a reason," said Moïse. "Sometimes they don't want to marry the person their family has chosen. Sometimes their father gave their land and animals to another sibling. So they have nothing, and they have to leave for the city. Sometimes they want to be an architect, but their family wants them to farm."

"Yes, I think there's a bit of that going on," I said.

"So I tell you: you will end up in Conakry. Everyone ends up in Conakry. I think the whole world goes to Conakry when they have nowhere to go," Moïse said, handing me a peanut. I waved my hand in polite refusal. Moïse shoved the peanut in his mouth instead.

"My family lives in the 12th century," I explained. "It's hard to connect with them. 12th-century Constantinople is a different world."

"Yeah, I understand. Don't worry, you will find friends in Conakry. My family also lives in the 12th century. Many people's families live in the 12th century," Moïse assured me, spitting the peanut shell out.

He continued: "You know, they want to help you, they're trying. But they don't have phones, they don't have TVs and radios. They work on the land and farm cassava. Or they tend their sheep and goats in the hills. They live like their parents and their grandparents. So they don't know anything about life in the city, they don't understand us."

"Is that how your family is?" I asked.

"Ehh, I was just making a general statement, you know. As an example, I mean," Moïse answered.

"I see. Just an example, right? They tend their sheep and farm cassava. Is there something else they do, up there in the hills, that you're not telling me about?" I asked.

"You know how to ask a lot of tricky questions," Moïse said, spitting another peanut shell on the ground. "Tell me about your village in Constantinople instead, is it also like that?"

"Yes in many ways, I suppose it is exactly like that," I said.

"Right," Moïse said. He handed me a peanut again, but then remembering I had already declined several times, dropped it back into the sack.

"My father is the Emperor there," I added after a while, in a more hushed tone, almost as a confession.

"Haha — so typical!" Moïse laughed.

"What?"

"My friend Ousmane is the same as you. His father is also a traditional chief. He's from the Tambacounda area. He's supposed to take over the chieftaincy," Moïse explained.

I mentally picked up my underwear from the floor after that rut, even though we were sitting on a stationary bench. The rut had also sent my father's imperial crown flying into a metaphorical sack of Moon Boké peanuts, but I was happy to leave it there.

"So is your friend Ousmane going to become a chief in Tambacounda?" I asked.

"Haha, no, he doesn't give a shit lol. He got a bunch of face tattoos and just wants to make death metal. We used to live in this basement together in Dakar. He's trying to jump-start the death metal scene in town," Moïse said.

"How is that working out?" I asked.

"You know, everything is possible in Dakar. I told you," Moïse concluded.

I looked up and grinned in bewilderment and comfort, imagining myself returning to Constantinople with a face tattoo and jump-starting the Byzantine death metal scene from the basement of the imperial palace at Blachernae, my father — the traditional chief — stomping on the floor to make me turn down the bass as my latest mixtape disrupts his meeting with the Venetian envoy.

I had a peanut after all and spit the shell on the ground.

6

A week after my father had summoned me into his office, I stood at the pulpit in the crowded palace church on the Feast of the Transfiguration. After the reading of the Scripture passage, I delivered the sermon I had prepared, as he had requested:

"God, in his love for us, made himself human," I said, "so that he could live through our pain and humiliation in this world, feel it in his flesh, and impart to us the certainty that, even in our lowliness, we are made in his image.

And so on this Feast of the Transfiguration, this warm and joyful feast, this day where the light of Tabor — the light of revelation — shines brightest upon us and stokes the fire of our holy Christian faith — on this day we, queer people, give thanks to God for not having forgotten us, and more: for having deigned putting himself through our experience during his sojourn on Earth."

I paused. I took a deep breath. Everyone took a deep breath. I touched my mouth mechanically. Everyone touched their mouth. I folded my hands on the pulpit. People craned their neck. I continued:

"As we pray for the Holy Spirit to come down and illuminate the allegorical meaning of Scripture for us, we see that Jesus put himself through the queer human experience three times. The first time was his baptism, which is an allegory of the process of coming out. John the Baptist did not change who Jesus was, he did not recruit Jesus into divinity, nor did he convince Jesus to reveal himself as divine. Rather, as a vehicle for the Holy Spirit, he triggered in Jesus the understanding of what he already was, so he could manifest to the world the reality of his divinity. This is an experience common to all queer people — a moment of epiphany, an uncloaking of a pre-existing truth. It is a moment of light, a moment of intense incarnation into our human bodies, where gratitude for the truth mixes with a sense of weight of the burden ahead."

A thin ray of light shone into the room, revealing specks of floating dust. I spoke louder and a bit higher:

"God is omnipotent. God did not have to go through baptism and epiphany. But God does not forget any of his creatures, and it pleased him to go through the process of coming out, and to know in his human flesh what queer people experience when their queerness is revealed to them and manifested to the world. For this, we thank our Creator."

The floating dust applauded in a silent festival of glittering micro-fireworks, as if excited by the light. Nothing else moved. I continued:

"Today's feast commemorates the second moment of epiphany in Jesus's life: his transfiguration — the further revelation of his identity. Scripture tells us that Jesus's appearance was transformed. His clothes became dazzling and his companions were terrified.

Now look at me, my friends. I have also transitioned and been transfigured. I have also emerged on an allegorical mountain for all to see, beaming with light and truth, my real identity revealed, my clothes dazzling, my companions terrified. And in this I am not alone, but rather one of the Lord's many trans creatures. For indeed it is the light of revelation — the one we call the Light of Tabor — that shines through our transitions, the same divine light that radiated from the transfigured Christ, and the same light that illuminated the apostle Paul when it dawned on him that he had already converted. Like us, Paul was cleansed of his former hatred, had to reconsider every aspect of his life, and came to the conclusion that truth lay not in following the law and acting according to expectations, but in accepting the light of God.

So on this Feast of the Transfiguration we celebrate the trans Christ — Christ transformed but unchanged, Christ revealed but transcended, Christ transgressive, transfixing, and dazzling. Our merciful God did not forget his trans flock. He did not have to be transfigured, but he chose to — and in doing so he reminded his trans creatures that they are made in his image, that his light shines on them, and that he desired to feel their experience in his flesh during his sojourn on earth. And for this, we thank our Creator."

The ray of light grew slightly wider and more diffuse. In the front row, a person's leather sandals glowed in the beam while their face remained in the dark. I continued:

"Long before Jesus came into the world, God inspired the psalmist to describe the dark side of our experience in Psalm 22, so that the experience of trans people in public places would be etched into Scripture: *I am scorned by others, despised by the people. Everyone who sees me makes fun of me.* This is the psalm Jesus invoked when he was on the cross, which is the third time he put himself through queerness. For even as he was hanging dying, he did not forget us. He was scorned by others, he was made fun of. He did not have to be mocked and humiliated, but he chose to feel our experience in his flesh. And at the paroxysm of humiliation and suffering, he committed his soul into the hands of God, and overcame the limitations of his earthly body, as we do when we transition. Dying on the cross, he transitioned, too. The body into which he had been incarnated was exhausted and shed, but the soul inside him persevered intact, destined to inhabit a resurrected body whose wounds are holy stigmata.

We come out, we reveal ourselves, we transition, and are transfigured. We are mocked, our bodies are mooted, but our soul continues intact, and our wounds become holy stigmata. Jesus did not have to experience these defining moments of trans life, but he chose to. He loved us so much that he wanted to feel our experience in his flesh. And he wanted us to know that we are made in his image. And for this, on this Feast of the Transfiguration, we, the transfigured, thank our Creator."

The light grew wider and dimmer. A sequined handbag shone faintly in the back row, then went dark. The floating dust stopped dancing. The incense stopped burning. The glimmer of the golden crosses stood still. The room remained silent. People looked at me in bafflement, their faces expressionless, as if it had just snowed in their bed.

I became intensely aware of my feet. A rooster was heard, far in the distance.

My father glanced at me from across the church, emanating the same manly resolve with which he had served pancakes to his soldiers on the walls of Dyrrachium and gifted the bodies of the city's young women to his Venetian contractors.

The air felt like it had turned to water, in a failed soggy eucharistic miracle. The fire had been snuffed — the congregation stood with their mouths open like a school of fish, still trying to suck holy incense into their gills.

It was clear I could not stay in Constantinople.

7

A man in a Led Zeppelin shirt jumped out of a minivan and asked me:

"Where are you going?"

"Conakry," I said.

"But what do you want?" he asked.

"Oh. Uhm. A van or car or any kind of vehicle would be fine, really," I mumbled.

"But why do you want to go to Conakry dressed like this?" he asked.

"Right. Well. I'm writing an imperial biography, you see, and…"

"In Conakry?" he interrupted.

Truth is, we're only halfway to Conakry and my project of an imperial biography is not doing well. Perhaps I need to sit down somewhere quiet and do some thinking about what I want. Perhaps this border crossing is a good place to take a breath.

A——CTUALLY NEVER MIND——————————!!!!
IT LOOKS LIKE WE'RE LEAVING RIGHT AWAY————!!!!
LOOKS LIKE MOÏSE HAS DISAPPEARED SOMEWHERE
PERHAPS HE FOUND ANOTHER BUS
OR: fellow angels
                         have already carried him to Conakry

iN A GOLDEN WiNGED CHARiOT.

I'll text him later.

UH-OH

So now I find myself in a **NINE**-passenger van, but so far only **SEVEN** travelers bought tickets.

You know what that means.

WEST AFRICAN MATHEMATICS COMPRESSES AND EXPANDS

DEPENDING ON HUMIDITY AND OTHER FACTORS

so we need to wait for another **NINE** to fill up the remaining seats until there's **395672453** of us then we're full and ready to go.

In Africa a lot of character development happens when everyone is stuck somewhere for hours in brutal heat. Moïse had been carried away by angels, so I was hoping they'd bring in a worthy replacement. I mean — I would, it's my story. Sorry, it's hot and I'm kinda dissociating.

As it happened, I sat in the front passenger seat next to a matron of some bulk wrapped in a dazzling gold, red, and green boubou with a matching headscarf, her bare feet on top of mine, her armpit nestled around my shoulder, her fingers dipping in and out of a Moon Boké peanut sack, her lips nonchalantly dribbling the shells onto my lap.

I left my door half open, pushing it wider whenever I needed more air, closing it tighter when bands of street children approached. I felt numb. I was slowly liquefying back into watery sand — but for the moment I was still inert and incompressible. I was prepared for a long, hot, featureless wait.

"What is this?" said the matron, grabbing my hand and frowning at my painted fingernails.

"What?" I asked weakly, without resisting her grasp.

"Your nails. This is not good for a man," she said.

"Well it's good for me."

"But it's not good for a man," she insisted.

"OK, well maybe I'm not a man," I said.

"Eeeehhhh???" she shrieked, dropping my hand.

She turned to the other matrons in the seats behind her. A lively conversation sparked up. Soon the whole bus was talking about me, my outfit, my nails, and what was good for me, all while dribbling Moon Boké peanut shells onto the floor.

I stared at the dashboard blankly. It was hot. I felt nothing, I had no thoughts and no emotions. I could not even muster annoyance or embarrassment.

"We are talking about you," she said finally.

"Mhm."

"Because we have heard about it, but we have never seen it."

"Mhm," I answered.

"We heard about it on the radio. But we have never seen one in person."

I didn't care.

I struggled not to float away into another dimension.

I said something, but I don't know what.

It was hot. I wanted gazpacho.

I had not consented to this conversation.

"Normally you are supposed to be stoned to death, because it is the law," she explained.

"And it is abominable," said a voice from behind, deploying the word "abominable" as if it had been waiting in storage for me.

"But since you're the first, we want to have a party for you instead," the first matron continued.

I drifted into exotic new depths of numbness and dissociation.
I entered a world of soft silent cotton
— where the universe is paused —
—

    the surreal,
    the tragic,
    the funny are all
        the same cloud-gray
            color   —

"So let's party!" she said. "Give us two thousand francs and we'll buy some drinks!"

"But I don't even drink," I said.

"But we do! We want to drink!" she said.

"Yes, we want to drink!" said another voice behind us.

At that point the whole world condensed into a hot van parked on a dusty border lot, and everyone was an African matron in a lurid boubou, and they wanted to drink.

And something was abominable.

And it was really hot.

I pulled two thousand francs out of my purse. She commandeered one of the street children orbiting the bus and ordered for drinks to be procured.

Meanwhile, a teenage girl approached me, a bucket of peanuts balanced on her head, and asked shyly through the window: "Are you a boy or a girl?"

"Give me some peanuts," I said, handing her a coin.

A few minutes later, plastic cups appeared, as well as a bottle of sparkling pineapple juice.

"What is your name?" she asked.

"Anna," I said.

"So we drink to Lady Anna! Cheers! This is your African coming-out party!"

Everyone in the van cheered and drank to Lady Anna's coming-out party.

I had a sip of pineapple juice.

it was overly sweet

it tasted somewhere between refreshing and poisonous

somewhere between poetic and prosaic

a liquid allegory for this moment.

"Now you are one of us, we will be your big sisters, and you will be our little sister!" she said.

"I'm glad," I said, like a clock telling noon.

My mind was somewhere else, perhaps turned off entirely.

I had left my body on autopilot on the passenger seat of a Guinean van.

It seemed to be doing fine fending for itself unattended.

There was no urgent need to reassociate and return to the world.

I fleetingly wondered whether I was expected to be grateful.

To whom?

For what?

It was too hot to be grateful.

FLUID STATES

8

Hours later we arrived at the bus station in Conakry.

"I will try to find some fish with rice," I said.
"Fish with rice! Come with us Lady Anna, we will find it, we are your sisters!"

Soon I was wandering around the vast muddy chaos of Conakry's outdoor bus station, carrying my own luggage as well as my big sister's — as was now my duty as a younger sibling — marching to the beat of the two matrons' decisive traipse across the labyrinth. We sat down somewhere. The elder matron promptly ordered three times fish and rice. There was no doubt I would pay for all three as the sibling who had achieved economic success abroad — as a Byzantine princess, no less.

The owner brought us a bucket of fecally contaminated tap water to wash our hands — and no soap, but three grimy spoons.

"I always bring my own spoon," said one of the matrons, dipping her spoon in the bucket. The other matron dunked her hands in the fecal bucket, then grabbed some vegetables out of my plate with her fingers. She tore some of her own fish into flakes and put it on my plate.

"This is a good piece of fish for you," she said, having restored the cosmic balance between vegetables and fish on my plate, as only a big sister could.

I felt a little light inside me again — like just a tiny lightbulb in a big dark warehouse, but enough to find my way into my body again.

"Thank you, Nafissatou," I said to the first matron.

"Finally I have a name in your story, eh?" she said.

I looked down but smiled.

Nafissatou continued: "You didn't use to have a name in my story either. As far as I was concerned, this was the story of *me* traveling to Conakry and meeting an exotic foreigner in wild clothing, and me having a learning experience. Remember this, Anna."

We ate with joy and appetite.

The Market Economy

1

My project of imperial biography has failed for multiple reasons:

— I've been disowned so there's kinda no point
— it's too hot
— dysphoria ys makyng me dyssociate and lose my gryp on realyty
— I'm in Africa
— I'm in Africa
— I'm in Africa
— hair

Let us return to the market in Ségou, since there is something inside we've been avoiding for about ninety pages, something about the deep dark mechanisms of power and violence, something about portals and intersections, something that requires performative political poetics, not narrative writing. Maybe they do witchcraft in there?

The market in Ségou is a poetry-only space. You can't come in if you're carrying prose. I'm sorry it took me a while to empty our pockets but we couldn't go in with so much prosaic baggage.

You also can't come in as a tourist. It's a marketplace, not a place for souvenirs and photo ops. It's the nexus where trade-offs are made, compromises are negotiated, life and death change hands, petty and grand things are transacted.

Take a break, get a drink, go to the bathroom if it's safe for you to do so.

When you're ready for that kind of space, turn the page, adjust your reading speed to "poetry" and join me in the market.

Floor 8.

At the market in Ségou, the eighth floor is the floor of shame.
It houses:
    menstruating women
    gay teenage boys
    apostates
    and people selling second-hand clothes deposited at charitable donation collection points in Europe.

Floor 9.

The ninth floor is the realm of weavers—all men.

Each weaver sits on a little stool inside a wooden scaffolding:

his legs are stretched out in front of him

the warp threads tied to a cylindrical—bar—across his lap

at one end

and to a counterweight far ahead of   his   fe$_{et}$

at the other end

a yarn cable is looped around ((each of his big to$_{es}$))

tied to an ^{overhead} pully

with one toe he pulls ha lf of the warp threads

down

throws the shuttle across the width of the loom—————

between the threads

—————————then repeats in the opposite direction

with the other to$_e$

each weaver keeps a reserve of

> chicken blood
> rice
> & kola nuts
> (for curses)

There is a master genie of weavers, called Jinn Moussa, who can be summoned for good fortune by declaiming a story in **metric rhyme** in the Fulfulde language. It must be

> IMPROVISED
> —and—
> MEANT IN EARNEST
> —and—
> IT HAS TO MENTION IRON
> —and—
> THE FLIGHT OF GRASSHOPPERS

The mythical ancestor of all weavers (called Diountel) can also be invoked by mentioning **God's mercy for the limbless snake.** However, he requires a different **metric rhyme** than Jinn Moussa.

Moral of the story: supernatural powers have **different poetic tastes.** Some tune into the **sound** of the phrase, others into its **imagery**. It is the **combination** of **meter** and **topic** that determines which supernatural power listens and responds.

On Poetry and Magic

I wonder if Hesiod and Sappho had something similar in mind. We readily extol *religious fervor* in our Christian authors, but *craft* in our pagan poets. And when it comes to those pagan poets, we carefully choose not to discern the power of faith in their words, because we only have one faith — in our Lord Jesus Christ — and we let all other belief be witchcraft.

We declaim meter and rhyme as critics and disregard the notion that their poetic technique may have had performative magic value.

But I wonder: do we fear catching ourselves summoning spirits we otherwise profess not to believe in?

My good master Michael Psellos alludes more than once to charms that work in our own Greek language much like Fulfulde magic verse. The keen reader of his *Chronographia* will find   Psellos   mincing around the
                                                       magic

              power of
              poetry as
              prior to him
              Procopius and
              previously
              Proclus and
              probably
              Porphyry and
              perhaps
              Plotinus all
              primly
              puttering   **AROUND**   the   topic
              pretending to be
              plodding about

        sense and
concept not
        sound but
collectively
carving out a hollow
        space shaped a lot like,
                well:
                      magic
     poetry.

```
┌─────────────────────────────┐
│                             │
│    (magic space keep out)   │
│                             │
└─────────────────────────────┘
```

So you see, not all invocations are for blessings.

Less benevolent genies can also be **DISCREETLY** called upon to interfere with competitors' looms and cause their threads to snap.

But for safety reasons I cannot say here how they are invoked.

Sorry.

If there is a line between folk spirituality and witchcraft, surely that practice crosses it, and it would be unbecoming of a Byzantine princess to be the herald of such unseemly pagan customs

///////\\\\\\\\
because propriety
\\\\\\\\V///////

However I can say that this is why the looms are arranged in a circle. The weavers look out the tower, with their back to each other, so they cannot see each other's mouth when they curse.

In olden times, the weavers did face each other

BUT

one day
a weaver named Amadou
—who was born deaf
                        but had grown up to be adept at lip-reading—
deciphered a curse
on a competitor's lips
which had caused his thread
                    to sna p!

Amadou exposed the culprit
who was promptly lynched by his colleagues
and beaten to death with a metal bar
        ow   bye bye

now

some weavers found Amadou's outrage out of place:
— why he did not invoke a counter-curse?
— was this call for justice was just a sign of him being a weak
    man?
— *etc.*

Moral of the story: men (imho) can be **trusted** to **challenge** each other's **masculinity** and flaunt their own in **every domain** of human activity, even witchcraft **smfh**

---

in any
                case some of the
            blood esca   ping from the offender's
              crushed skull   got
mixed with some of the
        chicken
            blood ke————————pt by other weavers for
               cursing   purposes
              causing disru ption of the entire
textile   production
      chain.

Then,

(later)

a weavers' assembly was <u>convened.</u>
a chicken blood bank was <u>proposed.</u>
as a means
to mutualize magical resources.
and to safeguard cursing supplies.
from contamination.
the project was <u>approved.</u>
facilities were <u>planned.</u>
with the
financial support.
of the
French Ministry of Cooperation.
but the

funds <u>disappeared.</u>   bye bye

during a power outage.
and to this day cannot be <u>located</u>

? ?

The weavers collectively decided that unfair competition needed to be:

    1) uprooted

or else:

    2) protected
    by guaranteeing the perpetrators' anonymity.

There was a general consensus that

fraud

itself was not a problem. It was the public disclosure of it that caused disruption.

> HARMONY CAN BE RESTORED BY LIMITING
> THE HARMFUL EFFECTS OF TRUTHFULNESS

Since that day the weavers have worked with their backs to each other in order to guarantee that saboteurs could work **INCOGNITO**. In coordination with the

floor of shame…♥

(just below)

,

it was also decided that concealing other scandalous practices was more beneficial to the community than eradicating them. And so **TWO DARK ROOMS** were built where the weavers could have **SEX** with each other **ANONYMOUSLY**. Because of demand and to avoid overcrowding on the

floor of shame…♥

(just below)

,

four more dark rooms were later built, bringing the total to six. Soundproofing was upgraded in all of them out of recognition that some men naturally orgasm more

loudly

(echo)

than others.

To this day a small fraction of the weavers' output is unofficially devoted to making tightly woven cotton condoms, often out of scraps, which are then discreetly left in the dark rooms as offerings from the community.

To accommodate the diversity of the masculine experience, the condoms are made in
two sizes
::

normal

which fits a human arm up to the elbow, and

small

which is approximately the size of a human penis and, more specifically, someone else's.

The small size is normally not used, except as a gift.
In either case the condoms are ceremonial and not worn during sex. Special curses are usually attached to them to cause pain or disease.

Moral of the story: because of their ability to simultaneously **foster** and **conceal** the practices of **witchcraft** and **sex between men,** the weavers of the ninth floor of the market in Ségou are often considered: - a **model** of a **self-regulating guild**
and have become: - a **standard case study** in **modern economics** textbooks

---

The same connection between **WITCHCRAFT** and **SEX** is found again on the sixteenth floor, which is devoted to herbs and pharmaceuticals. On that floor, an entire aisle is devoted to magic powders and decoctions that *magically*…♥ cure hepatitis and AIDS.

That aisle is informally known as "weavers' aisle," though in practice it is equally frequented by their infected

> wives
> mistresses
> and prostitutes
> (with some overlap)
> the issue is these groups
> keep getting bigger because
> of the spreading of the infection
> and the secrecy surrounding practices
> that contribute to unchecked contamination
>
> …

It is one of the two places in the market with a true diversity of genders, ethnicities, ages, and social classes.

The other is the sixteenth basement level underneath the market, where users of these medical powders and

> decoctions are
> dumped in a
> dank unmarked pit when they
> die.

bye bye

Following local pharmaceutical practice, they are dumped through a secret chute

.

.

.

.

.

.

.

(thud)

, their names forgotten
, and their bodies consumed by:

goblins.

I should add that I did not personally visit the soundproof dark rooms—it would have been unbecoming of a Byzantine princess to eavesdrop on the privacy of orgasming men.

But I was warmly invited to do so seven times during my visit on this floor:

1) once by a shy young weaver named Adama who said "take me with you" before proposing a visit to the dark room;

2) a second time by a bearded man called Moussa, a father of three, wearing a skullcap and embroidered white robe, who asked me several times with insistence "so you are a woman, right?" before suggesting the dark room;

3) a third time by an unnamed wiry older man who came to sit next to me while I was writing in my notebook and fondled his genitals through his robe while assuring me I wouldn't be disappointed by the size of his penis — until I told him to

go because I was busy writing this book and could unfortu-
nately not give him the attention he required;

4) a fourth time by a cheerful and self-confident young man
   nicknamed Pigeon Voyageur — I did not learn his real
   name — who promised me sex with him would be quick and
   he "just wanted to try";

5) a fifth time by a sweaty visiting government official in an ill-
   fitting suit who said he would have his personal chauffeur
   pick me up and take me out to dinner afterward if I let him
   penetrate my body;

6) a sixth time as a fleeting hint by a weaver called Zoumana,
   who said "we do have the dark rooms if you want the complete tour — I mean, OK, it's fine we can also stay here";

7) a seventh time by an anonymous young man who did not
   say anything but motioned at me with one index finger re-
   peatedly going in and out of a ring formed by the fingers of
   his other hand, while winking and nodding his head in the
   direction of the dark rooms.

I count myself lucky to have been the object of so many displays
of spontaneous hospitality in a foreign land, and as a historian I
feel a duty to record for posterity how warmly a Byzantine princess can be received in these parts of the world.

Floor 10.

The tenth floor is where the strips of woven cotton are sewn together into wider sheets.

It takes:

1	strip of woven cotton to make a normal size condom;
2	to make an embroidered skullcap for the devout men who wear them;
4	to make a chic boubou that won't stain when they fondle themselves through it;
8	to make a prayer mat in a corner of a soundproof dark room, just in case;
16	to make the outer lining of a hair elevator;
32	to make orgasm-grade soundproofing panels for public dark rooms;
64	to make gears and cables for all-cotton elevators in town markets;
128	to make Moon Boké peanut sacks for a year's worth of daily peanuts per household;
256	to make a complete 1997 Toyota Corolla, including cotton tires and windshield;
512	to make a cotton cow to sacrifice to cotton gods in the cotton hills above Nzérékoré;
1024	to make cotton cities ruled by fabric republics floating on cotton oceans;

and more for planets moons and asteroids.

All those things are sewn on the tenth (10th) floor.

Floor 11.

The eleventh floor is the realm of dyes.
It is a world of
      hanks and coils and skeins
      and vats of murrey and madder and wattle and woad
      and kegs and tubs
         of cudbear and cutches
         and orchils and galls
      and looms of bogolan
           dunked in indigo.

Floor 12.

On the twelfth floor is a blind man called Ibrahima, who is a griot and the market administrator. In addition to having memorized the Holy Quran by the age of ten, he also knows everyone's name and phone number by heart, and also their father's name and phone number, and also their grandfather's name and phone number, and in some cases each ancestor's name and phone number for dozens of generations as far back as the invention of names and phone numbers, and even before.

Floor 13.

The thirteenth floor is the world of *gara* —
a Bambara concept that encompasses —
         — asthma inhalers
         — caustic soda
         — sodium
           hydrosulphite.

This floor extends indefinitely into all directions
and covers the entire surface of the Earth —

It is connected to the floor of dyes, two levels below, by (about)
twenty PVC pipes:

—
—
—
—
—
—
—
—
—
—
—
—
—
—
—
—
—
—
—
—

Down on the eleventh floor, yards of cotton soak for days in
bright vats of indigo.

But indigo is not soluble in water because it was discovered by
a clan

whose symbolic animal is

the cat

and cats are afraid of water

To this day indigo still does not spontaneously bind to cotton
fibers.

In order to make it water-soluble, indigo requires a reducing
agent, which makes it lose an electron

(bye bye)

this is done by piping caustic soda and
        sodium hydrosulphite
                down from the thirteenth floor.

through the (about) twenty PVC pipes:

—
—
—
—
—
—
—
—
—
—
—

113

On the thirteenth floor

those two substances are stored in giant donut-shaped soft plastic containers

disposed concentrically like huge circular sausages

one circular sausage of caustic soda

then an empty space

then around it a huge sausage of sodium hydrosulphite

of bigger diameter Ø

then a bigger empty space

then around it a sausage of caustic soda

of even bigger diameter Ø

then an even bigger empty space

<——and so on outward indefinitely——>

Some of the bigger outer rings
of soft sausages of chemicals
partially float on the ocean
~*~*~dolphins play around them~*~*~

the ones that pass through the vicinity
of Mecca and Jerusalem are

o-O-o-O-o-O-o-O-o-O-o-O-o
objects of devotion
o-O-o-O-o-O-o-O-o-O-o-O-o

along their———entire circumference

with:
annual nautical pilgrimages
far out into the open sea
—|||||—to touch the floating plastic tubes—|||||—
and silent prayer sessions
about topology
and connection with holy ground
and sermons on geometry
and sausages

~**V**__**V**__**V**__**v**__held on the deck of oceangoing ships

On the eleventh floor, dye workers spend their lives
elbow-deep in indigo
their hands and arms are dyed dark blue

Ndomadyiri

(the fourth manifestation of God)

is responsible for this:

he gave humans agriculture
and revealed the dyeing power of indigo

—to the cat clan—

but in exchange for this knowledge
he made their hands
forever the color of the deep dark night

so that at every instant of their life
they would be reminded of their finiteness.
constant indigo blue on their hands,
they contemplate   at   all   hours
the eventual recycling of humans →
back into immaterial ←
spiritual
beings
after their work on Earth   bye   bye
and their passage
            —through→
                  various stages of initiation

The completion of the whole spiritual cycle is

SYMBOLICALLY REENACTED

by dumping water tainted with:
- ✓ indigo dye
- ✓ caustic soda
- ✓ and sodium hydrosulphite

into → the ground

EVERY TUESDAY NIGHT

There it enters the ecosystem and the water supply, where it is absorbed by:
- ✓ fish
- ✓ birds
- ✓ reptiles
- ✓ insects
- ✓ small children

IN COMMUNION WITH THE COSMOS

Ndomadyiri gifted

COTTON

to humans   (well thank you)

now

the spiritual primacy of

COTTON

over synthetic substances

is CELEBRATED IN ALL TOWNS AND VILLAGES (yay)

by keeping:

A PERPETUAL FIRE

continuously fed by:
- ✓ plastic bottles
- ✓ plastic bags
- ✓ polyurethane foam (from discarded furniture)
- ✓ broken PVC pipes
- ✓ shredded tires.

The mystical fire produces:

	carbon	nitrogen	hydrogen
SOOT	X		X
CYANIDE	X	X	
ARSENIC	*(do you know that one?)*		
BENZOPYRENE	X		X

as offerings to Ndomadyiri

(well thank you)

Those are not consumed by him directly, but by:
- ✓ fish
- ✓ birds
- ✓ reptiles
- ✓ insects
- ✓ small children
      (on his behalf)

IN COMMUNION WITH THE COSMOS

once

indigo dye=====binds=====to the **COTTON** fibers

it has to be

to become water-insoluble
(again)

and ensure the color$_{fast\ n\ e\ s\ s}$ of the blue $^{c\ l\ o}$ t h

this is done by exposing the freshly dyed

fabric to the AIR

1) at first it is

PALE YELLOW

2) then it turns

LIGHT GREEN

(it===binds===with electrons *pulled*

from atmospheric oxygen) $=$ O

3) then

DEEP EMERALD GREEN

4) then

BRIGHT BLUE

5) then

A RICH DARK BLUE

On the thirteenth floor

        the empty space   s

between the plastic sausages of

    a)   caustic soda and
    b)   sodium hydrosulphite

are devoted to the allegorical representation of this

    a)   spiritual and
    b)   chemical

progression—i.e.,

    a)   increasing blueness and
    b)   **UNION WITH THE COSMOS**

this is left to small children

by exposing them to the contaminated **AIR**
they follow *the* cycle of indigo *and* become *more* and *more* blue
with **asthma**…..

On the **OUTER RINGS** of the thirteenth floor the children
are>>>

p a l e >>>>>>>>>>from breathing **soot**

CLOSER TO THE CENTER they turn>>>

light green>>>>>>>>>>from breathing **cyanide**

CLOSER STILL inorganic microparticles in the air make
them turn>>>

light blue>>>>>>>>>>from **lack** of oxygen

CLOSEST TO THE CENTER they are>>>

>>>>>>A RICH DARK BLUE>>>from the final stages of>>>asthma

in each ring there is an **increasing** number ####### (of)

plastic asthma inhalers of

different colors and **vintage**

arranged in LaRgE-sCaLe patterns

not immediately discernable to the naked eye (tho)

towards the center there are oooooo = no children anymore, only:
a large pile of used asthma inhalers.

(bye bye)

The inhalers that complete that stage of mystical initiation and have finally freed themselves of their children owners (bye bye) are thrown into the great fire and transfigured into:

ᴀᴛᴍᴏSPHERIC NANOPLASTics

+

their guiding spirit chemical (usually arsenic or formaldehyde)

The arrangement of the successive rings of plastic sausages interspersed with

a)   increasingly blue children
b)   rows of used plastic asthma inhalers
creates a pointillistic pattern
that cannot be apprehended

at

eye

level, but it is said that from space it looks like an Adidas tennis shoe. Some say that it is a message for visiting aliens telling them what deity we worship

others call it a coincidence
others yet think it looks more

like:
    a cucumber
    a nail clipper
    —or—
    a tea kettle   who knows
                                ¯_(ツ)_/¯

2

I texted Moïse: "so u know the whole story now"

He texted back: "lol 12 century drama"

Then a few seconds later: "#conakrylife"

I smiled, put my phone away in my purse, and watched a seagull gracefully dive into an overflowing trashcan and ree-merge triumphantly with a little piece of fresh rotten something. For a moment I felt myself soaring peacefully above Conakry and having a picnic on a rotten cloud with the friendly seagull.

(well thank you)

Bobby texted me

whats up "sis"……

did u
did u rly
did u rly need to
did u rly n
did u
ass
asshole
assh
did u ha
did u have to
did u
d
weree
were the
were the quotat
were the quotation ma
were the quo
were
w
do u

hey bobby
Sent

also
"cis" urself jackass

lol
hows everything

fine

where r u now

africa

what century

21

lol ok
is it safe there

no
i mean kinda

africa not safe for queer folx

meh

but ur still alive

somehow

so whats keeping u safe

being a rich white foreigner obv

lol thats cool

uhm
i didnt ask for that privilege

but its keeping u safe tho

its literally keeping me alive

so whats wrong w that

if i was from here id get beaten up

ye

but if i was home i would also get beaten up
and privilege wouldnt keep me safe
it only works here

how do u feel ab that

rly not sure tbh

but its working out for u

i dont have a choice
this is what i got
#intersections

dude
ur like herodotus

dude
dude

sry

also herodotus came back

ur not coming back?

to what

ig

so whats new in 12th c byzantium

whats new in 12th c byzantium
lol nothing ever by definition

hello coinage reform??

mhm ye coinage lol

well say hi to dad

uhm….

or not

ye stay safe ttyl

I met Moïse the following day around dinner time.

"My project is in disarray," I said. "I set out to compose an imperial biography but now the circumstances hardly call for that. I'm disowned, I'm in exile…"

"Hahaha no shit," Moïse laughed. "And you think I'm the angel figure in your story who guides you through difficulties and shows you the way?"

I wanted to say "oof" but quickly closed my half-open mouth before the next cosmic rut, then remembered we were not in a moving vehicle so I let it gape silently. I mentally picked up my underwear from my floor.

"Well thank you," Moïse said before I could answer anything. "Princess, buy me some cow meat," he continued, "I think you can afford it. Your father is a traditional chief in your village and probably has a huge herd. You didn't tell me this but I'm guessing."

"Sure," I said.

We wandered a bit and found a suitable cow meat establishment. Moïse ordered a greasy soup full of tendons and tripes and cartilage and muscle, like a veterinarian anatomy book artfully melted into a bowl. I ordered some rice and vegetables.

"This is really good, princess. Are you sure you don't want to try it?" he asked.

"I imagine it's very good but you know I don't eat meat," I said.

"I know, but you're missing something," he said.

"So why are you in exile?" Moïse asked after a while.

"Well I just told you the whole story, didn't I?"

"No, no, you told me why you're in Conakry. But why is this exile to you?" he asked.

"Uhm. Well. Because I'm not… from here?" I offered.

"I'm not from here either, I'm from Nzérékoré. I'm also new to Conakry. I also don't speak their local language or know their food. I've never had a soup like this," Moïse said.

I said nothing and prepared myself once more for my under-wear to end up on the floor, and for the entire crown jewels of the Byzantine Empire to end up in a sack of Moon Boké peanuts.

"So how is this exile to you, princess? This is not exile to me. This is really nice. We're in Conakry, we're having cow meat, this is as sweet as life gets. We're in Conakry, princess, in Conakry! Do you even realize what that means! Endless possibilities! You probably still can't believe that you're here," Moïse said.

"I suppose that part is true," I conceded.

"The spell is broken," Moïse said beaming.

"Which spell?" I said.

"I thought you had guessed already," Moïse said.

"I figured there was something of that order, but I haven't guessed anything. Do you want to tell me?" I said.

"My parents were rich," Moïse said, "but that was probably obvious to you already."

"No it wasn't," I interrupted. "I'm probably missing half of the things that everybody says and does here in Africa. That's what it's like to be foreign."

"Haha, OK. Well," Moïse smirked. "Anyway, my parents were rich before I left Nzérékoré. They always had a good cassava harvest, and we had lots of food at home, even meat. Can you imagine, princess? I grew up eating meat all the time. That's how rich we were. I don't know if you can imagine it."

"There are a lot of things I can't imagine, Moïse," I said. "But go on."

"My father wanted me to stay. And farm and harvest. Not just in Nzérékoré, but really with them at home, and just farm cassava. He wanted a young strong body to produce more and more cassava. And sell it on the market. And make more money. And buy meat whenever we wanted. And buy a television. And shoes for everyone. And a water tank. He wanted to live like a rich man," Moïse explained.

"And you didn't want those things?" I asked.

"I did, but not at the cost of spending my whole life farming cassava to buy them," he said. "I wanted to live life. To see things. Maybe to study something. To meet people, you know?"

"All reasonable things. We all want to live and not be part of someone else's project," I said.

"Anyway, we argued. And I left. And so my father put a spell on me to punish me and make me come back," Moïse said.

"And what was the spell?" I asked.

"I think you're going to laugh," he said.

"I'm ready," I said.

Moïse smiled, then explained: "he sacrificed a cow to the ancestor spirit of all cows, who lives deep in the forest above Nzérékoré, and proclaimed that I would never eat cow meat again in my life, and that no man or woman in the world could ever break that spell."

I burst out laughing so hard I nearly snorted half a spoonful of rice.

"Hahaha, this is amazing," I said finally.

"Yes, it's amazing," Moïse said, now also laughing.

"And you needed to run into a nonbinary Byzantine princess to break the spell," I chuckled.

"My father said 'no man or woman in the world.' He didn't say anything about nonbinary Byzantine princesses. You're neither a man nor a woman, so you can break the spell—and you did. That's what he gets for being an out-of-touch cassava farmer and coming up with stupidly worded spells, it's entirely his fault, haha," Moïse said, chortling, holding his spoon full of cow meat like a mystical trophy, a scepter of protein victory over the forces of darkness.

"I guess you never know what you represent in someone else's life," I said.

"You never know," Moïse said, triumphantly slurping a cow tendon into his mouth.

"So now you see, princess, I'm not in exile in Conakry," he continued. "This is where I'm finally free, after a long journey to earn that freedom and break what was holding me back."

"I see it now," I said.

"Tell me the truth, isn't Conakry infinitely more exciting, more open, more diverse, more modern than your village in Constantinople?" Moïse asked.

I chuckled, first with irony, but then without: "Actually. I mean... Actually yes. It is. It's also amazing that I'm here. And I guess I chose to come here, just like you did. And... to be frank I came with a fair bit of excitement. I didn't come here reluctantly."

"So we're not in exile. We're just in Conakry," Moïse said,

"But I'm still disowned," I said.

"Of what?" he asked.

"Of the Empire. Of the legacy of my father," I said.

"Am I also disowned?" Moïse asked.

"Well, uhm, I don't know how it is with your parents now... are you?"

"No, no, I mean, am I disowned of those things you just mentioned: the Empire, the legacy of your father?" he asked.

"I guess... I guess not? In fact, no, obviously not. Definitely not." I said.

"And why not? Why am I not disowned of the Empire and the legacy of your father?" Moïse asked.

"Well there was never any expectation that you would inherit those things in the first place, I suppose?"

"Exactly!" Moïse said. "I'm from Nzérékoré, I'm not from your father's tribe, he obviously wasn't planning to pass his land and his herd of animals down to me, and I wasn't planning to go to your village in Constantinople to tend his herds and take care of his elderly wives. So I'm not disowned."

"Indeed none of those things had any chance of ever happening — for perhaps many more reasons than you think. So maybe it's all a matter of expectations," I said.

"Yes," Moïse said. "We're both new to Conakry, we each have our baggage, but as far as I'm concerned I'm not in exile and I'm not disowned, and it's really up to you whether you're in exile and disowned. It has to do with your own expectations of what was supposed to happen."

I looked down at my bowl of rice while Moïse slurped another tendon with even more gusto.

"Hahaha!" he laughed finally, "you're totally going to make me that angel figure who guides you through tribulations and shows you the way in your story, aren't you? I can totally see that, it's written on your face, princess, hahaha."

"Maybe?" I smirked. "My original project is dead. But I'm a historian and a chronicler, and I don't know what am I going to do, so angels are always good. Also, I'm the spell-breaker in your story, so it's totally fair that you can be the angel in mine."

"So find another project. Be a historian in Guinea and Mali. You're here now. There's no shortage of stuff to write about. Write about the historical dimension of you being here. Connect to this place like it was already here before you showed up, instead of floating through it like it's just the backdrop of your exile," Moïse said.

"I see what you mean. I wrote an article about the weavers of the market in Ségou. I originally thought I might send it to my little brother Bobby, who doesn't know much about economic policy and will need this kind of scholarship to help him run the Empire — since that's the plan now," I said.

"Princess," Moïse interrupted me, "maybe leave the Empire alone? Why don't you write *for* me and *to* me, instead of *about* me for the benefit of the Empire and your relatives back in your village in Constantinople? Remember what Nafissatou said when you had dinner with her: she has a name now. She's not just a learning experience in your story anymore. You probably have a role in her story, too. Maybe her family had a curse about fish, you never know."

I nodded.

"The market in Ségou is not just an object of scholarship for the Empire's policy, it's the center of the magical universe," Moïse continued. "And you already know that. You already wrote thirty pages of magical poetry about it. And *in* it."

I put my spoon down.

"You thought this was an imperial biography, right?" Moïse added. "But now your book has become about giving up on that project, because you're not even part of that power structure anymore. You're disowned from it. Then you thought maybe this could at least be a juicy travelogue for the benefit of your friends back home in Constantinople, didn't you? But instead, you're coming out as a poet of African magic and politics. We're going to have to leave your relationship to Africa undefined for now. You're not African and you're not in exile either. You're a rich white itinerant transgender Byzantine princess in an endless liminal space. Every step you take is going to keep you in that intersection of power, politics, poetry, magic, and history. You're going to need to write another book just about that. You can't even give up on being a historian, you need to be one. Just not of your father, that project was dead before you even started. That imperial glory is dark. It's dark for me and it's dark for you. But we have plenty of other dark things here for you to chronicle if you're going to be a poet of dark magical–political spaces. You can be a historian of African liminal spaces."

I looked at the ceiling. The bulb was broken and it was dark, but I could see a spider in the corner rolling up a fly in a silk shroud.

"You're playing that angel part perfectly, Moïse," I said finally.

"Haha," Moïse laughed, "if you're going to make me an angel in this story, then I'm going to come back with my angel squad in the last chapter and take you up to the roof of the market where there's divine light, and we're going to show you some serious Guinean-style Christian redemption and transfiguration lol."

3

Anna Comnena,
"Nash Equilibrium in Magical and Semi-magical Environments"

The Journal of Magical Economics 21, no. 5 (2020): 52–57.

Game theory is a computational model for the study of complex interaction strategies under magical and semi-magical constraints, originally developed by Mohammed Bagayogo and his disciples at Timbuktu's Sankoré University in the latter half of the 16th century. Bagayogo called it *nadhariat ul-laabati* after the Arabic expression for "theory of games," but these days it is simply known in Bambara as *nassariatou*. It has many applications, from divination sciences to astrological systems, and more recently nonlinear sorcery.

A key concept in *nassariatou* is the notion of *tawazun*, also called "Nash equilibrium" after the 16th-century Songhai mathematician and theologian El Hadj Seydou Touré Nash. The regulation of sorcery among the weavers of the Ségou market is one of the oft-cited examples of *tawazun:* the weavers vie for a finite set of customers, but also benefit from a fair and safe workplace. Given these constraints, they can either compete or not compete, and if they do compete they can do so fairly or unfairly.

The optimum equilibrium would be a cooperative state, where all the weavers pool their resources and output, sell their wares to customers as a collective entity, and redistribute the economic proceeds equitably within the cooperative. But this equilibrium would be jeopardized if any individual weaver bypasses the cooperative and sells to customers directly, increasing his profit beyond what the cooperative redistributes to him. Every weaver would have an incentive to engage in such disloyalty, unless there was strict enforcement and the risk of severe penalties for disloyalty. So this equilibrium is not attainable in practice.

Another possible equilibrium would be fair competition, where the weavers are permitted to have individual customers. They would have an incentive to work hard and make good products, but with protection from unfair practices like magical sabotage. This would benefit all the weavers, since their labor could be entirely devoted to making good products and keeping customers satisfied. But again this ideal equilibrium is unattainable; each weaver has an incentive to betray his colleagues and reap the benefits of feeling safe in his own work, while secretly sabotaging everyone else's work, so that the benefit of the safe environment only accrues to him.

In the first case—the failed cooperative—cheating does not reduce the weavers' collective wealth. However it causes it to be unevenly distributed among weavers.

In the second case, disloyalty does reduce the weavers' collective wealth, but that situation can be corrected by smashing the offender's skull with a metal bar, so that potential cheaters integrate the cost of death by cranial trauma into their risk calculus.

In real-life situations there is not always a metal bar lying around, or people may have really hard skulls made of anodized titanium, or some weavers might have a personal distaste for blood and gore, etc.

That is why *tawazun,* the so-called Nash equilibrium, is the only possible solution. Weavers all engage in magical sabotage, don't get caught, don't crush each other's skulls, but spend a lot of time and resources hurting competitors or mitigating damage inflicted by others. This behavior reduces everyone's wealth, and results in both individual and collective loss and waste of resources. Such is the weavers' guild at the market in Ségou.

Reality is more nuanced. Recent *nassariatou* research out of Mali's leading game theory departments tends to critique the traditional Bagayogo analysis of the Nash equilibrium at the market in Ségou along two lines. The first one—typical of progressive scholars in the field of magical studies—is that is this view of *tawazun* is human-centric and only considers the gains and losses incurred by the weavers, while ignoring the incentives and behavioral patterns of the spirits being invoked.

Nonlinear sorcery has emerged as an academic field largely out of the need to quantify and model the incentive structures of magical entities: spirits, jinns, ancestors, etc. While there is a centuries-old body of knowledge on how to invoke those entities and put them to work for the benefit of humans, research has only just barely begun on understanding what motivates those magical entities to cooperate with humans in the first place. More research is needed to understand what spirits ultimately want, how they determine the value of offerings and sacrifices brought by humans, and whether concepts developed for humans, such as "wanting" and "needing," are relevant when describing the behavior of magical entities.

An emerging body of scholarship suggests that the most promising conceptual tools combine economic analysis with poetic analysis. Supernatural powers have different poetic tastes and appreciate different kinds of magical poetry. Some tune into the sound of the phrase, others into its imagery, etc. For example, it is often the combination of meter and topic that determines which supernatural power listens and responds. The correlation is well documented, but it is still unclear whether supernatural entities appreciate magical gestures for their poetic value, or poetic gestures for their magical value.

A second line of critique on the traditional Bagayogo game theory analysis of *tawazun* is that it assumes materialistic goals. It takes for granted that only economic gain or loss has a value that can be computed. That assumption leads to a seemingly irrational result at the Ségou market, where the weavers apparently all lose and collectively settle for an inferior equilibrium that makes everyone worse off. This analysis regards the practice of sorcery as a wasteful expenditure of resources that causes economic loss for both perpetrator and victim.

While there is no debate that it causes economic loss, scholars of sorcery (both traditional and nonlinear) have pointed out that it may also result in a non-economic immaterial gain. Indeed, it may be incorrect to assume purely materialistic goals when analyzing magical and semi-magical market dynamics—and perhaps West African micro-economic systems in general—and perhaps any system where poetry, magic, and economics interact.

Some scholars have proposed a possible type of non-economic gain: cultural prestige derived from demonstrating expertise at magic. But this analysis still assumes a materialistic environment. Cultural prestige may only be a proxy for a value that can later be parlayed into economic gain. Nonlinear sorcery can, here again, be credited with a bolder approach. It attempts to model a genuinely non-materialistic environment, where the practice of magical poetry and the interaction with magical entities is not a means to ultimate gain (economic or cultural), but is itself the reward.

That newer model turns the traditional economic analysis of game theory on its head. It refuses the implicit cultural hierarchy that views economic gain as the primary motivator and non-economic gain as secondary—in other words, as mere currency that can be cashed into economic gain. On the contrary, modern nonlinear sorcery considers economic equilibria from the perspective of *portals*. It assumes that the greatest desire of the weavers of Ségou is access to the supernatural world. They achieve that access by engaging in a poetic practice that opens up a portal to a spiritual dimension.

In this newer paradigm, economic gain is only desired to the extent that it can ultimately be parlayed into access to the supernatural. If wealth can secure a portal into a supernatural dimension, then it is desirable. But if it cannot, then it is either useless or a waste of resources that could be more directly put to magical use. This model correctly predicts that the practice of poetry is more likely to create portals to magical dimensions than the accumulation of wealth. It also correctly predicts that the players in the game are more likely to find an equilibrium where poetic practice is maximized, because it increases opportunities to access the supernatural.

Thus this new analysis reveals that *tawazun*—the seemingly irrational Nash equilibrium reached by the weavers of Ségou—is in fact entirely rational. It is a perfect equilibrium from the perspective of magical game theory. The weavers have maximized access to the supernatural—which is their highest reward—by creating an environment where the practice of magical poetry is not only facilitated, but made necessary.

The weavers of Ségou have also reduced the spiritual waste created by the pursuit of unnecessary economic gain. Instead, they have collectively settled on a lower economic equilibrium that equitably reduces wealth for everyone. Non-materialistic market dynamics are self-enforcing and protect individual weavers from the temptation of wasting resources on economic gain since those gains are unattainable.

Instead, each weaver is placed in the position of constantly having to engage with magic and maintain a praxis of contact with the supernatural. This involves poetic craft as well as real-time economic analysis of the value of poetic sound vs. poetic imagery. This, in turn, maximizes both individual and collective spiritual gain and fosters the collective maintenance of portals into magical dimensions.

4

My project of imperial biography is going very well after all!
I set out to learn about men and power so I could write about
daddy, and I found there's different flavors of his ilk:

1) the big macho man like Ivorian president Houphouët-
   Boigny, who does the theft himself but delegates the murder
   part to underlings;
2) the warrior-king type like Bohemond of Antioch, who does
   murder hands-on but farms out theft to his subordinates;
3) the market economy of Ségou, where murder and theft are
   systemic and highly distributed between lots of little men
   who make little individual contributions to that dark system;
4) and...

... at the pinnacle of it all, the Byzantine Emperor, who com-
bines all the features of the above: a master of both theft and
murder, who can expertly do both in person without delegating,
but is also the head of an economic and political machine of
theft and murder—called the Empire—where little men can get
a chance to participate in the greater system of darkness. All of
that masc engineering apparently involves hair, power, murder,
witchcraft, and supernatural portals.

5

Magical–political darkness can be exported far and wide if you know how. In Ségou, the fourteenth floor of the market houses the sales department, where bogolan cloths are separated into three piles:

1) those destined for local consumption,
2) those for export to other African cities,
3) those for overseas export.

Bogolans intended for local consumption need to be magically solid so they can be used as protective garments in contexts where blood is involved, such as hunting and circumcision. But the fashionable metropolitan shoppers of Dakar, Abidjan, Accra, and Kinshasa have no interest in bogolan magic. They just want a chic textile to wear in night clubs and restaurants, so they can look rich and get laid. They demand the pieces with the finest cotton, the most flawless craftsmanship, the best executed and most intricate designs. The most expensive bogolans of all are the deep black or very dark brown ones with thin white patterns, and perfectly regular lines. Those are the ones you can wear while holding a glass of champagne.

Irregular bogolans with dyeing or weaving imperfections—or those with crude designs made by apprentices—are sent to Europe, where white hipsters have entirely different requirements. They look for poor craftsmanship as a sign of African authenticity, and wear bogolans in solidarity with the Third World.

Savvy wholesalers in Ségou cater to European tastes by buying large batches of blank undyed gray bogolans at a lower price, ordering blue, red, and yellow industrial chemical dyes from Germany, and hiring local children to make random patterns in bright solid colors on the cloths. Those garish multicolor bogolans are then sold back to Germany, where shoppers find the bright colors and random patterns more African, and buy them for higher prices than the traditional designs.

A company in Shenzhen, China, makes "Fair Trade" labels—printed in twelve-point `Courier` font on off-white cardboard—for 20,000 CFA francs a box of 1000 labels. These labels are attached to each bogolan before it is shipped to Germany, which doubles the retail price.

A True Story

On the Silbersteinstrasse in Neukölln, Berlin, a man named Dada from Ibadan, Nigeria, started selling bogolans in the back of his internet café and telephone shop after hearing about them for the first time a few months ago on the "Nigerians in Berlin" Facebook group.

He printed a low-resolution picture of his aunt Folu making spaghetti bolognese in her kitchen in Ibadan from her Instagram feed, cropped out the spaghetti, and glued a copy on the back of each "Fair Trade" label.

The resulting connection with a GENUINE AFRICAN PERSON has proved so rewarding for German shoppers that Dada has been able to raise prices by 20% since coming up with the idea. He hasn't told aunt Folu about using her likeness to promote his business—but has mentioned that GOD HAS BEEN GENEROUS in providing for him, and has started sending her eighty euros each month from the WesternUnion branch around the corner, along with requests for continued prayers.

(well thank you)

6

One of the frustrations of Byzantine history is how seldom power tools come up—but I'm here to change that. I also told you we'd be back for more elevator visits, so here we are.

In the elevator

In the center of the market building in Ségou is a giant elevator. In theory, we didn't need to go through all the floors one by one, but you and I know that we actually did.

The elevator rises through all twenty-six floors and even goes a few more floors up into the void above the building, past the roof, where there is only wind and vertigo. It also goes deep into every underground level beneath the market: parking garages, septic tanks, sewer systems, and even a bit further down into the ground below the building foundations, into the upper layers of underworld where there is only death and darkness.

It is very slow because it is made of cotton (even the gears).

To go up, you have to take the stairs to the desired floor and staple the cotton walls of the elevator into the wall of the elevator shaft, using the very large diesel-powered staple gun that is normally chained to the inside of the cabin. If it's out of staples, then the elevator is out of service. It is not unusual for it to run out of staples: government officials have been known to skim the staple supply for their own private consumption, or to divert it to lesser staple-powered elevators in their native province in a misguided act of nepotistic patronage.

It's very rare that the staple gun is deliberately stolen or damaged, but Ibrahima, the administrator and market griot on the twelfth floor, records two such occurrences in the history of Ségou. These are the momentous events I will now endeavor to recount in this elevator chronicle.

In 1810, the Peul imam Sékou Amadou, returning from jihad in the newly established Sokoto Empire, rode into Ségou on a gray horse, followed by ten thousand heavily armed disciples. These men were trained both in the physical rigor of the battlefield and in the intellectual rigor of the *madrasa,* and that's exactly how bad things happen to elevators. Sékou Amadou defeated the Bambara ruler, declared an end to animistic practices that he deemed counter to the Holy Quran, and crowned himself Emperor of Macina as well as *Amir al-Muminin,* or "Commander of the Faithful."

Sékou Amadou's first act as Emperor was to forbid the use of ostentatious objects, even in worship. The great mosque of Djenné was closed for being too grandiose, and the great market of Ségou was stripped of the hallowed staple gun that had been chained inside its elevator for generations. That ancient staple gun, made of ebony inlaid with ivory, was never recovered—but to this day it is celebrated in pop songs worldwide.

The second time the staple gun was deliberately removed from the elevator was on March 10, 1861 at the Battle of Ségou, when the advancing forces of the Toucouleur jihad led by the sufi imam Oumar Tall forced the Bambara royal family to flee to the walled city of Hamdullahi. The Bambara king, Ali Diarra, had just enough time to collect the staple gun and the rest of the royal treasure and cart it off to Hamdullahi in a caravan of thirty-eight camels. Then Ségou was overwhelmed by the Toucouleur, and Oumar Tall proclaimed himself caliph on the roof of the market, as one does.

Both the Toucouleur and the Bambara were defeated shortly thereafter by the colonial French army led by general Louis Faidherbe, and the staple gun was packed up in a trunk and shipped to Paris together with the rest of the Bambara royal treasure.

To this day it is exhibited on the third floor of the *Musée de la Grandeur de la France* in Paris as item #84829B with the following label:

Objet rituel (?) usage inconnu — Afrique de l'Ouest
— fin XIXe siècle (?)

*Ritual object (?) unknown usage — West Africa —
end XIX century (?)*

A new staple gun was then made by the guild of Ségou staple gun craftsmen, more beautiful still than the previous two, and that's the one still in use today.

When the staple gun is operational, it is used to staple the cotton wall to the cinder blocks of the elevator shaft. Then boiling water is poured into the elevator shaft until everything is soaked, including the cotton wires, cables, and gears. For practical reasons, the elevator is only used after heavy rain, so water can be collected on the upper floors in specially built clay tanks. There is no running water in the building, and thus no other easy way to bring a lot of water up the stairs.

Once enough water has been collected and the rain has stopped, great fires are lit underneath the clay tanks and the water is boiled before being poured down the elevator shaft. The hot water causes the cotton to shrink, which is how the elevator cabin moves. The process is very slow, since cotton does not shrink as fast as mechanical elevators can move. It also works better empty: loads can stretch the cotton back into place and prevent the elevator from shrinking enough to reach the desired floor.

The weight can also cause the staples to fail and the whole elevator to tumble down the shaft into the bowels of the earth. For all these reasons the elevator is rarely used, and it is considered largely ceremonial. Even when it is used, riders are advised to run it empty and take the stairs to meet the elevator at its destination while it slowly shrinks into place.

In any case, the current staple gun is made of orange thermo-plastic (specifically, acrylonitride butadeine styrene), inlaid with glass beads and sapphire. Its diesel motor is said to be carved out of a single solid piece of ebony, but it is not visible because it is covered by zirconium-plated steel plate, locked in place by a rotating pearl. The whole device is tied to the elevator cabin by a heavy gold chain. The top of the staple gun used to have a Manchester United sticker but it has been partially removed and is now only recognizable to elevator scholars familiar with that type of iconography.

v

Airtime

1

With each new epiphany, each new transfiguration, each new birth and crucifixion — at every liturgical feast the brutal African road consecrates — my lightly worn imperial underwear ends up on the floor, and my dad's imperial crown in a sack of Moon Boké peanuts. What is it with men and crowns and peanuts? Would it all make more sense as an anime series?

Sometimes clarity comes from Guinean television. I had to meet Moon Boké.

MoonTV is headquartered in an unassuming building in the Kipé Kakimbo neighborhood of Conakry, on the right-hand side of a broad nameless boulevard, between the Jehovah's Witnesses' local Kingdom Hall and Restaurant Le Bambou.

Half of the boulevard is closed off as Guangdong Construction Engineering Corporation technicians dig, grade, and pave all the way from the center to the airport. Overhead a banner proclaims:

Habits must conform to norms, and norms must become habits.
让 习 惯 符 合 标 准 ， 让 标 准 成 为 习 惯

A little cinderblock shack, jutting out into the unevenly tiled front yard of the MoonTV compound, houses the building's receptionist. A guard sits alone in the shade on a chair in the yard, checking his phone, his machine gun resting on his lap.

"Are you here to see the boss?" the guard asked while I put my phone away.

"I think so," I said.

"He will come down for you in a second. Have a seat."

I sat down on a maroon velvet armchair, facing a faded portrait of president Alpha Condé in full state regalia, an old fire extinguisher, and a large wall map of Guinea on which the town of Boké was covered by a Manchester United sticker.

Elhadj Boubacar Camara — better known as Moon Boké — was a spiritual leader, a traditional healer, and also one of the richest men in Guinea and the owner of MoonTV, which is what had brought me here. Soon I would meet him in person and we'd talk about peanuts, underwear, redemption, and of course making an anime series.

Moon Boké had made a fortune growing peanuts, marketing them in sacks of 1 kg, 5 kg, and 20 kg all over Guinea, then slowly diversifying his activities to include electronics, public infrastructure works, traditional healing, and now television. I only knew him from YouTube videos, where he appeared riding into town on a white horse after riots, appeasing the angry populace with carefully chosen holy verses and sacks of peanuts.

I wasn't quite done with the mystery of charismatic men and their peanuts. My own father had wangled a dubious dodge out of the musty grasp of the unwashed, sweaty, savage Bohemond of Antioch. I needed airtime, not answers.

I sat quietly counting coins until the elevator door opened and Moon Boké appeared.

"It is so nice meeting you!" he said.
"Likewise, thank you for having me here," I replied.
"Let's go to my office and you can tell me everything about what brings you to Conakry," he said, ushering me into the elevator. I gathered the folds of my dress and stepped in. The doors closed behind us.

In the elevator

i'M
    curiOus
        tO hear
            hOw you like
                cOnakry
                sO far
is this   yOur first time visiting Guinea?
                dO
            yOu
        knOw
    anyoNe
    here
 ?
You can tell me about it when we get to————>my office
This elevator is a little s l o w :
                        haha
(but we'll get there)
Also, we have so many floors now
                every year we add:
                            a few
when I started   My TV channel
                let Me tell you —
            it was just Me
                and My secretary
i had to do everything   Myself

                it's not so easY
        running a TV channel bY
                        Yourself
                especiallY
            in this countrY
                        You know
but the thing is — Guinea reallY
                        needed another TV channel

of course we have government television,
                        and people watch it
and it's good, no I mean, it's good
(don't get me wrong)
but   — how can I say?

                I felt like I could offer a different perspective

"On the 16th floor we have our special dubbing studios, do want
to take a look?" We stopped on the 16th floor. The doors opened
with a little ding. I peeked out. It was completely dark. The doors
closed again.

what I've been doing is showing old American series
and we get good numbers
— yeaaaah — good numbers   01234567890 = +++
the old ones from the 1990s are cheap

I buy them in bulk — in bulk! BULK BULK BULK
I run them all day — all day
like nonstop nonstopnonstopnonstopnonstop nonstop

but now — now — I want new contents!
I feel Guinea is ready for new contents — really new contents
and I'm going to bring it to the country((←

I want to do documentaries
?
we have the capability right here in house — yes
what if we did a documentary series on Byzantine coinage?
HAAAA that would be brilliant!
how do you like that idea?

I know you love it
I can tell you love it
you're smiling =) (: (= =) :) (=   !!
eeeeeehhhhhh we're gonna do Byzantine coinage!!!!!

we're going to be the only TV channel in West Africa with that contents

THE ONLY CHANNEL IN WEST AFRICA WITH BYZANTINE COIN-AGE

our enemies will not even understand what is happening to them!!!

       i Mean
     in terMs
      of Market share
    and sheer MASS————————————>penetration

"Do you want to see our news studio on the 23rd floor? Come, let's take a look!" We stopped on the 23rd floor. The doors opened with a little ding. I peeked out. It was completely dark. The doors closed again.

Anything they can do — we can do.
All in house, right here — yes
My secret weapon is my son Lamine!
He is only 16 but he knows everything about computers.
Everything. His name is Lamine.
He is like our main engineer. Did I introduce you? His name is Lamine.
Why do I need to hire an engineer from Europe, you know?
Europeans are so expensive.
They want pomegranate dispensers everywhere.
They're coming for the money, not to hang out in Conakry.
You still haven't told me what brings you to Conakry?

"Do you want to see our special effects lab on the 29th floor? I know you want to see it! Let's take a look!" We stopped on the 29th floor. The doors opened with a little ding. I peeked out. It was completely dark. The doors closed again.

I've really enjoyed our conversation
Let's have dinner together tonight
Do you want to have dinner together tonight?   nom nom

I'll pick you up at your hotel
Downtown in Almamiya?
Yeah it's called Almamiya   yes
Do you know who that neighborhood is named after?
Sékou Amadou, the first Emperor of Macina.
He called himself *Amir al-Muminin,* or "Commander of the
Faithful."
Which turned into Almamiya.

His first act as Emperor was to forbid the use of ostentatious objects, even in worship. The great mosque of Djenné was closed
for being too grandiose, and the great market of Ségou was
stripped of the hallowed staple gun that had been chained inside
its elevator for generations.

We'll talk about it over dinner!
I'll pick you up at 7 pm.

2

In the end it was decided that MoonTV would produce an erotic gore anime series, but with a Byzantine coinage subplot. It would be titled *Commander of the Faithful: Masks of Transfiguration.*

Episode 1.

Folu, a seamstress in Ibadan, Nigeria, finds a Mossi mask in a can of bolognese sauce while making spaghetti. The same day, she receives eighty euro from her nephew Dada in Berlin with the mysterious message "God has been generous." The mask is painted dark red with white stripes. Folu weaves a braid out of dried spaghetti and attaches it between the mask's horns. The mask turns out to be attracted to dust and clouds and perpetual motion. It wants smoke, smells, drifty wafty drafts and things.

Meanwhile in Conakry, Nafissatou has just returned from the market in Ségou and is telling her family about drinking pineapple juice with a transgender Byzantine princess on the bus. As she opens a 5 kg sack of Moon Boké peanuts [product placement opportunity here], she finds an ancient Baoulé mask. It is made of shiny black ebony, with bulging conical eyes, little crosses carved under its eyes, no mouth, and a chiseled frieze all around its face. In the following days, as she tries to feed the mask and care for it, she discovers that it's attracted to palm fronds and coconut rustles. It seems to be a consumer mask that just wants wealth, with no emotions and no goals.

Episode 2.

In the 11th century, a fierce battle is taking place in Dyrrachium between the forces of good (the Byzantines) and the forces of evil (the Normans). The scene is pink and soft and fluffy, and all the characters are stuffed animals: rabbits, warthogs, monkeys, shrimp, and lobsters. Gratuitous gore scene, guts, blood, etc. The head of the bad guys, Bohemond of Antioch [stuffed animal tbd — lobster?], retreats to his tent and masturbates. Long, detailed, gratuitous cum shot scene, etc. He ejaculates a non-Newtonian fluid whose visco-elastic properties change under shearing stress — peanut butter or hair gel tbd [product placement opportunity here?]. Make him look vulnerable to appeal to emo audience.

The Byzantines win the day by making pancakes with maple syrup. But their coins are debased because the gold contents has dropped so much. One type of flat disk brings victory (pancakes) but another type brings despair (coins). A fluffy pink stuffed rabbit has a long monologue over the resulting cosmological imbalance, introducing the coinage reform subplot. The monologue is in metric verse and first mentions iron and the flight of grasshoppers, then God's mercy for the limbless snake. It turns out to be not just narrative, but performative magical poetry. By the end of the episode, Jinn Moussa, the master genie of weavers, and Diountel, the mythical ancestor of all weavers, have both been summoned to Dyrrachium. Both of them are fluffy pink stuffed animals. Cliffhanger!

Fan Service (ファンサービス) Notice

Following long-standing anime practice (erotic gore anime being no exception), it was decided that a certain amount of material would be added to the series for the purpose of servicing fans, i.e., pleasing the audience and making it drool in anticipation of the next episode.

In terms of market segment, *Commander of the Faithful: Masks of Transfiguration* is more geared toward the chemical engineering fan crowd, so episodes typically involve hot chemical engineering scenes as a nod to that subculture. Even the action surrounding the coinage subplot offers gratuitously erotic footage of alloy fabrication.

Real-life audiences watch anime for entertainment, and would rather watch scenes of hot metal bonding into coins than intrigue about monetary policy. Trust me, that's a fact, I've been in television long enough.

Episode 3.

The butch blond Bohemond, bearing a Bambara bogolan and a Baoulé mask, does bukkake on beautiful blind Byzantine bishōnen boys in a bauxite mine in Boké.

Three little pigs — Porphyry, Proclus, and Procopius — perform Peul prosodic poetry while preparing peanut pomegranate pancakes [possible product placement opportunity?].

An angry old griot grooves over ground grains and grieves in great detail over a graceful old phonograph while everyone agrees.

Back in Dyrrachium, corruption creates a critical crease in screen craft and accounts for a crack in credibility that crystallizes as crinkly ochre corduroy in the crucible of narrative clarity.

The systematic alternation of voiced and unvoiced alliteration unexpectedly summons an unidentified sibilant liquid spirit — plot twist!!!

Episode 4.

In this episode, it is revealed that the narrative plot is archetypal, contains no suspense, and is in fact subservient to the deployment of sensory and emotional stimulus. That stimulus provides the energy for controlled trespass out of the mundane and into the supernatural.

Supernatural spaces in West Africa are metaphysical cracks in the universe, which provide an interval for collective healing and affirmation. Their gatekeeper spirits are like the Greek muses — mystical beings powered by the collective poetic imagination and kept alive by performative theater. They have individual poetic tastes. Some tune into the sound of the phrase, others into its imagery.

The richer the sound and the imagery, the wider the portal into the supernatural space. Even chemical engineering is an element of performative poetry. It is a tool for controlled dissociation. Like time travel, it works by dissolving the immediacy of the present into a puff of disembodied archetypal symbols. The metaphysical breeze oxidizes it, removes its corrosive aspect, and makes it harmless, allowing it to bind with the gist of other places and times, so that it can precipitate wherever and whenever.

On Transfiguration

the trans time traveler is a MASTER PRACTITIONER of
transfiguration

THEY'RE   the archetypal trespasser
        an intrusive audience
            that walks on stage
                (performative theater but open parentheses
        then… collective ANXIETY

            bc ROLES & SCRIPTS are all ¿?¿?¿?

THEY'RE   a fugitive performer
    i. walks off stage when provoked
    ii. goes to sit in the audience
    iii. opens a bag of popcorn mid-sentence

THEY'RE   the magical interfering with the safety of the
                                    technical
                /slash the technical interfering with the safety
                                    of the magical
                /slash
                /slash

THEY'RE   poetry that rips at   prose
                            like leprosy
                                and prose that
                dribbles gravel into
                    lyrical fluff till it's
                                ruff

THEY'RE   perennial transgressors
       dwelling in   ( )   X   ( )   i̶n̶-̶b̶e̶t̶w̶e̶e̶n̶ spaces
renting a hotel room on a cloud of trash ~~in the sky~~
and taking the bus————————————————————>somewhere else

Explanation: they practice transfiguration as a **refuge** and **dissociate** fluidly into the safety of metaphysical cracks like a non-Newtonian **alloy** of clear liquid, solid metal, and plasma.

THEIR HOME   is an elevator
(Ding—) :
an oppressive rancid-smelling box that, through the joint power of technology and poetic imagination, carries with it the promise of opening up onto a gentle utopia that is always moments away from becoming real.

Episode 5.

This episode is devoted to a staged metric reading from John Conteh-Morgan's 1994 article "African Traditional Drama and Issues in Theater and Performance Criticism" on a plain background in MoonTV's 23rd floor news studio by Moon Boké's 16-year-old son Lamine, wearing a furry rabbit costume:

"In [African]   Cultures,
                    Characterized by normative and

                            Sometimes highly
                            Stratified

                            Social

                            Structures,
Individual   Conduct and
Inter-group relationships are less a matter of
                            Spontaneous and natural
Interaction than of   Conformity to a
                    Codified mode of behavior,
            to what
                            Some role-theory
                            Sociologists have aptly
                  Called a '
                            Social script.' this '
                            Script,' present to be
                            Sure in all human
                            Societies but particularly
In evidence in traditional African
                            Societies where it allows
for far less
Improvisation,
Is actualized in a variety of ways.

Chief among these are
Symbolic movements
and actions,
Stylized gestures,
patterned dances,
and even
Speech, which is often
molded into a
variety of
Fixed
Forms,
Formulaic expressions, and tropes."

A carrot is used instead of the microphone. Lamine occasionally says nomnomnom between the lines.

On West African Social Theater

The white foreigner is a standard stock character of West African social theater. They come in several archetypal variants, such as the unfashionable, highly gendered straight expat with a lot of local knowledge and the more fashionable but less knowledgeable consumer–tourist. Both are rich, socially prestigious, and powerful. The character of the white foreigner speaks in the first person in West African theater — in stock phrases, like all the other characters — but centered around their own wishes and desires. They appear in archetypal dialogue with a certain class of African characters: street vendors, guards, taxi drivers. Associating with the white foreigner character brings prestige — and possibly wealth. However, they bring prestige of a material kind, associated with the world of consumption and institutional leverage — as distinct from the kind of immaterial prestige associated with a religious leader, a healer, or a member of the traditional aristocracy. In that domain, the prestige of the white foreigner is low.

The transgender princess is also a standard stock character of West African social theater. The archetype of that character is fashionable, and perhaps vaguely magical, but cloistered at home and invisible. They are poor, powerless, and have low social prestige. Associating with that character brings shame — and possibly poverty. The character of the transgender princess doesn't speak in their own name, they only appear in the third person in the speech of others — and often in sentences where their existence is denied, yet alluded to.

But the transgender princess character also carries the unique prestige of abnormality and transcendence, a quality that brings no wealth and no social recognition, but leaves open the poetic possibility of acess to liminal spaces and supernatural portals. This is why the transgender princess remains a stock character of West African social theater, and is not just expunged. They do not represent the expression of an individual's identity (which is not the goal in West African theater — there are only stock characters), but are an allegorical incarnation of a societal kink, a collective dark side that just had to materialize somewhere. They face violence, but only to the extent that the collectivity directs that violence toward itself, in frustration at its own dark side, in a botched attempt at self-exorcism, and not as punishment for that individual's transgression.

What West African social theater lacks is the character of the white foreign transgender princess. That character would combine incompatible dramaturgical features: a third-person character that only exists as a secret precipitation of collective chemistry, but also a first-person subject whose wishes and desires drive the action. How could those be the same person? It also cannot be introduced, because stock characters only emerge out of the collective imagination.

When that impossible character actually appears on the street and needs to pee, dramaturgical chaos ensues. Characters forget their lines, mopeds drive into lampposts, ontological planes crash into each other, unguarded portals open up between centuries, elevators, and consonants — at the risk of uncontrolled transfiguration.

Episode 6.

Seydou the money changer is strolling along the piers of the Conakry harbor. With him is his 16-year-old computer genius son,
Lamine. At the end of the episode, it will be revealed that he is
also Moon Boké's 16-year-old computer genius son Lamine (plot
twist).

But for now he is staring at the ocean, his eyes drowned in
hazy reverie. He can see sweltering swamps, crocodiles, yellow
and purple birds. Somewhere really far and really hot, with fist-
sized insects — Constantinople perhaps.

The young Lamine is thinking about the concentric sausages
of caustic soda that go through Conakry and jut far out into the
open sea. He's imagining, one day, going on a nautical pilgrim-
age to touch the floating plastic tubes: the silent prayer sessions,
the connection with holy plastic, the romantic sermons on geometry held in the open air on the deck of an oceangoing ship…
Emo close-up on Lamine's face. Big eyes. Teen heartthrob vibe.

Episode 7.

Whooshing zoom intro shot, down from the cosmos into a little
alley in Yamoussoukro. Chantal is grilling rats — big rats — small
rats — medium rats. K-pop vibe: fresh costumes, diagonal shots,
close-ups of smiling grilled rats, people moving in sync around
the outdoor kitchen, rats cooking in sync, flipping at the same
time. Close-up of tails, snouts. A 1997 Toyota Corolla parks in
front and revs to generate diesel fumes. Christmas music from
the car stereo. "Romantic sunset in diesel haze" vibe, blueish
light, possible product placement opportunity: the 1997 Toyota
Corolla can go a million miles on a single oil filter, etc. "What do
you want?" sings Chantal.

At this point, reintroduce the Byzantine coinage subplot.
One customer wants to pay for their grilled rat with a gold *no-*

misma in the effigy of Emperor Michael IV the Paphlagonian. Another one pays with a slightly concave alloy *hyperpyron*. A discussion ensues: Why is it concave? Why is it an alloy? Why the effigy? What do they want?

Plot twist: Chantal's kitchen is also a forge, and the coins were minted right here. She doesn't just grill rats, she also smelts metals at the same time, and alloys of different substances, even — on request — alloys of metals and rats. At the end of the episode, we understand that the imperial Byzantine mint is right here in an alley in Yamoussoukro.

Episode 8.

In this last episode of the season, Seydou the money changer returns for an exclusive live televised theological interview with me — only on MoonTV.

SEYDOU   Princess, I thought about our discussion on Byzantine coinage back at the border. I have revised my position. I think my comparison was incorrect.

ME   Which one?

SEYDOU   My idea that your father's coins are like my father's sheep, and that he mixes different kinds to make them stronger.

ME   And why have you changed your mind?

SEYDOU   Because your coins have the effigy of your traditional chief on them. Our sheep don't have anyone's effigy.

ME   And why is that significant, in your opinion? Because sheep are living beings but coins are inanimate objects?

SEYDOU   No. In fact my concern is that it's precisely the opposite.

ME   Namely?

SEYDOU   That your Byzantine coins are not inanimate objects.

ME   But instead?

SEYDOU   That they are not equivalent to our sheep, but to our
         masks.
ME   How so?
SEYDOU   African masks are not inanimate objects, you already
         know this. They are supernatural portals to spiritual
         spaces. The Baoulé mask in the hair elevator in the
         basilica in Yamoussoukro is not decorative, it is a
         portal to local earth spirits. The kind who have with
         no mouths, who mutter in palm fronds and coconut
         rustles, and just want wealth. And the Mossi mask…
ME   Yes, I remember. But coins? We use coins daily for
         trivial things. But do you really use masks daily? As
         magical portals? And for trivial things?
SEYDOU   Islam forbids it.
ME   But do you?
SEYDOU   I think I have answered your question.
ME   I think you have. And so have the weavers of the
         Ségou market, now that I think of it.
SEYDOU   Now what about your coins? Do you use them as
         magical portals?
ME   I don't think so, but I'm willing to be shown wrong.
         Portals to what?
SEYDOU   Byzantine spirits.
ME   I'm not sure we really have those. Isn't that an African
         analysis of our Byzantine culture?
SEYDOU   Then what is it that Michael Psellos, Proclus, Pro-
         copius, Porphyry, and the   others keep alluding to
         and dancing around without mentioning it?
ME   Whatever it is, our religion forbids it. We only have
         one faith — in our Lord Jesus Christ — and we hold all
         other beliefs to be witchcraft.
SEYDOU   I think you have also answered my question.
ME   I think I have. I also thank you for asking it.
SEYDOU   So do you Byzantines fear catching yourselves sum-
         moning spirits you otherwise profess not to believe
         in?

168

ME   I see your point with Psellos and the others. But with
          coins?
SEYDOU   Why do your coins have the effigy of your traditional
          chief?
ME   The Emperor's face on currency represents wealth, the
          Empire, paternal authority, continuity.
SEYDOU   And what are those?
ME   What do you think they are? Spirits?
SEYDOU   Evil spirits. Very evil spirits. Demons.
ME   Worse than the Baoulé spirits who demand wealth?
SEYDOU   The Baoulé at least understand what their masks do.
          They know what they're doing when they contact
          spirits. They know what the spirits want. They have
          spent centuries developing a practice of spirit man-
          agement. They have a complex initiation system to
          restrict access and mitigate risk.
ME   But the Byzantines?
SEYDOU   You don't even know what you carry in your pockets.
          You think they're just coins. You are carrying the de-
          mons of wealth, Empire, paternal authority, continu-
          ity, with you everywhere you go. You haven't even
          acknowledged the presence of those things, much
          less their power over you, much less begun to manage
          them. You don't even understand what they want
          from you.
ME   And what do they want in your opinion?
SEYDOU   Human lives and suffering.
ME   What makes you say that?
SEYDOU   Where are the young women of Dyrrachium that your
          father sold? Who did he sell them to?
ME   The Venetians?
SEYDOU   The Venetians just did the earthly job. That's not
          whom he sold them to.
ME   So then?
SEYDOU   Wealth, Empire, paternal authority, continuity. That's
          who consumed those lives.
ME   And what else do those evil spirits want?

SEYDOU Child sacrifices.

ME Child sacrifices! I don't think anyone in Constantinople sacrifices children. I have never heard of it.

SEYDOU Then what brought you into exile here? Why are you
on Guinean television and not at home making death
metal in the basement of your father's palace? You are
the first born, why are you not running your Empire
like your brother Bobby? Who sacrificed you?

ME I guess the man on the coin.

SEYDOU And to what?

ME To those demons you mentioned, you're right. I see
it now. And to one more, that you didn't mention,
but that thrives in their presence and demands child
sacrifices.

SEYDOU Which one?

ME Gender conformity. Queerphobia and its many sinis-
ter faces.

SEYDOU See, you know the demons of your own civilization
very well after all. You know their names, their faces,
how they are related to each other, whose blood they
demand, and who sacrifices victims to them.

ME I guess you're right. I know them. I have always
known them. They thrive in the shadow of our Christian religion, like flies on livestock.

SEYDOU My father raises sheep in the hills of the Fouta Djalon.
Beautiful, strong, healthy sheep. But no matter how
well he tends the sheep and how strong they are, the
flies come back. It is a never-ending task to keep them
at bay.

ME At least flies don't demand child sacrifices. Our demons do. They suck love out of families like leeches.
They are parasitic demons who use crude camouflage.
They pose as God, wearing masks, and divert his love
and his light away from his creatures, in an act of
spiritual corruption.

Zoom out. The screen goes blank, then dark. End of season 1.
Credits scrolling:

MOONTV CONAKRY PRESENTS
COMMANDER OF THE FAITHFUL: MASKS OF TRANSFIGURATION
EXECUTIVE PRODUCER: ELHADJ BOUBACAR CAMARA
WRITTEN AND DIRECTED BY: ANNA COMNENA
VISUAL EFFECTS AND ANIMATION: LAMINE CAMARA

3

THE INTERNATIONAL JOURNAL
OF AFRICAN ANIME

Review of
Commander of the Faithful: Masks of Transfiguration

by Ibrahima Kouyaté, administrator of the Ségou market,
historian, and griot

I have enjoyed the first season of MoonTV's new series *Commander of the Faithful: Masks of Transfiguration,* and I would particularly like to comment on Episode 5, and especially on the idea of the white foreigner as a standard stock character of West African social theater.

In the early history of West African contact with Europeans, especially with the Portuguese in the 15th and 16th centuries, the majority of white visitors to Africa were people who were marginalized in their own society: Jews, petty criminals, *degredados, lançados.* The dynamics of oppression in their home community gave their oppressors a pretext to push them out, and also gave the oppressed a good reason to leave and come here to Africa. They ended up here not because of what Africa had to offer — which they usually knew little about — but because it was far from Europe.

Once here, they fared variously. Some remained steadfast promoters of the Empire that had pushed them out, some married into aristocratic African families and integrated into our communities, some took advantage of their intermediary position to engage in trade, including the slave trade, and some did all of those things at the same time.

What all of them had in common is that their marginalized status was neutralized in Africa, and in fact compensated by their status as exotic white visitors. 15th- and 16th-century West Africans had no preconceptions about the antisemitic power dynamics of Portuguese society. What they saw was a white person with strange clothes, strange manners, and a strange language, and probably would have had a similar initial impression of a dispossessed Jew in exile as of a privileged Catholic prince.

What these early European visitors didn't know — but soon discovered — was that our West African societies are pluralistic, and always have been, and that being a foreign visitor was perhaps not that exotic. The character of the dispossessed stranger in exile who arrives in a new community after a long journey, with strange clothes, a strange language, and no knowledge of local customs, had already been a staple of African societies since long before the first Europeans arrived. So is the scenario of that stranger finding a space in local communities and assuming a specific role as a stock character in African social theater.

"Finding a space" in the context of our West African societies doesn't mean ignoring differences and pretending that everyone is the same until the stranger is no longer a stranger. In fact, as the Peul proverb says: *Ko wi'i fow no fota, ko no komo janforee* — "claiming everyone is the same is a trick to cheat naïve people."

No, it means, on the contrary, finding a theatrical space with a role to perform within the ongoing play of African social theater, even if that role is that of the "the outsider," or "the marginalized stranger in exile." That integration is a dramaturgical accommodation that accepts the marginalized stranger as an archetypal character, regardless of who that stranger is. It is not a manifestation of empathy and hospitality toward an individual.

Our own classical Bambara theater often features the archetypal character of the Dyula trader in the role of "the outsider." That character is mocked and caricatured, just like Jews are mocked and caricatured in 16th-century Venetian *Commedia dell'arte,* but in both cases the mockery confirms that "the outsider" is very much an insider, and an essential character in a theatrical system — albeit in a perpetually orbital role.

The inflexibility of West African social theater, with its strictly defined roles and scripts, is also its flexibility. Nothing new disrupts it, novelties get subsumed into existing archetypes, newcomers always find that they were expected, and that a costume was already waiting for them — not because each of them is individually greeted and welcomed, but because the play already had a role for an outsider even before the actor arrived.

And so the specific character of the white foreign transgender princess might be new to African social theater, but the general character of the marginalized white person in exile — who comes to Africa and thrives in the orbit of our societies because their marginalization is neutralized by their privilege here — is not new. It is in fact so old and archetypal that it might even be called a classical character of African social theater.

Over the centuries, it has appeared in many different avatars on our shores. Just in Mali alone, Christian and animist white Berbers fleeing the arrival of the Arabs and of Islam came to us across the Sahara. The *Tarikh-as-Sudan* chronicle reminds us that the 11th-century founders of our Zuwa dynasty were not Africans, but refugees from Yemen. Another chronicle, the *Tarikh al-Fattash,* tells us that some Jews persecuted in Spain settled near Timbuktu in the 14th century and amassed considerable wealth there. Our own Dyula traders may be perennial outsiders in Bambara society, but their wealth as tradespeople gives them privilege — and therefore safety — in our poor and agrarian societies. And in the 15th century a different group of persecuted Jews, from Portugal this time, began arriving on the shores of what is today Senegal and Guinea Bissau.

Structurally, it stands to reason that the people who have the greatest incentive to attempt a long and difficult journey, and to seek comfort and prosperity as outsiders in an unfamiliar society, are the ones who are marginalized in their original communities — and not the ones whose privilege already gives them adequate comfort if they stay put.

The character of the marginalized white visitor is therefore a separate variant of the "white visitor" character, distinct from "the tourist–consumer" or "the expat" and its many versions (aid worker, teacher, missionary, businessman) — and indeed not welcomed by any of them — but equally archetypal as them.

And so I argue that we have been expecting the white foreign transgender princess's visit for centuries, and that there is already a well-worn classical costume and an ancient script ready for that marginalized stranger in our social theater. The script is clear: to be in the role of "the outsider" that gets mocked, which in Africa also leaves open scenarios like starting a dynasty, acquiring wealth, or being beaten to death. The exact outcome depends on an imponderable element of improvisation by all the actors involved, as always here.

As with Dyula traders in Bambara theater and Venetian Jews in the *Commedia dell'arte,* the play is not about celebrating "the outsider" and inviting their inclusion — quite the opposite. But systematic rhetorical mocking is at least a standard form of dramaturgical integration into our theater and makes the character part of our universe.

Whether that role is comfortable for the actor is another question — nobody said it would be. But then again, whether any of the roles in all of West African social theater is comfortable for any of the actors, including local ones, is also debatable.

4

At 7 pm I went down into the lobby of my hotel and texted Moon Boké I was ready. I also borrowed the hotel's staple gun, having left mine in my room.

Finally Moon Boké texted back:
"omw" (in French of course)

I gazed fixedly at my phone and at those mystical letters etched in black on a light gray screen — like healing verses from the mouth of a marabout. Their casual sparkle seemed so transcendent and poetic in the desolate maroon plastic wilderness of the hotel's lobby. I looked up and saw a beaming portrait of president Alpha Condé in full state regalia, a bright red fire extinguisher, and a large wall map of Guinea on which the town of Boké was covered by a Manchester United sticker.

Finally at 9:45 pm Moon Boké walked in, followed by his assistant Béatrice.

"Hehehe I was delayed! This is my assistant Béatrice, by the way!"

We filed out of the hotel onto the street and into Moon Boké's colossal SUV — the holy man at the wheel, myself in the front passenger seat, Béatrice in the back.
"Béatrice is my assistant, I don't think I've introduced her," he said, while turning into a busy one-way thoroughfare in the wrong direction. He continued:
"Also, my sister lives in Canada. Did I tell you my sister lives in Canada?"
"I'm sure you did," I said.
"Do you want to talk to her? She lives in Canada. Let's call her!" he said, fumbling to dial her number on the dashboard

screen while barreling down against traffic across downtown Conakry.

A cyclist carrying eight 5-kg sacks of Moon Boké peanuts threw himself into a street vendor's tomato stand to avoid the oncoming luxury missile. Meanwhile the car's eight speakers played five consecutive dial tones in full stereo.

"Boubacar!" said a voice.

"Hey sis!" said Moon Boké.

"Sis yourself, jackass!" she laughed. "Where are you now?"

"I'm driving down the Boulevard de la Corniche."

"Haha, the wrong way again?" she asked.

"It's a long detour otherwise," he said.

"Boubacar…"

"Listen am I not the president and founder of West Africa's most innovative TV channel? I think it comes with certain privileges. I can drive wherever I want."

"Boubacar…"

"And speaking of which, listen, I am going to dinner with a Byzantine princess!" he said, then turning to me and whispering: "Come on, say hi!"

"Καλημέρα!" his sister interjected before I could say anything.

"Χαῖρε!" I responded with surprise. "Where did you learn Greek?"

"I used to live in a Byzantine neighborhood in Toronto," she said.

"Ah really? Amazing! I had no idea they had a Byzantine neighborhood," I said.

"They have everything in Toronto. Did you look?" she asked.

"I guess not. I didn't look for Byzantine neighborhoods in Toronto," I confessed.

"See? You gotta dig into the reality instead of making assumptions," she said.

Moon Boké interjected:

"We're gonna get some fish! Let's talk soon, sis!"

He hung up. The dial tone played five times in full stereo through the car's eight speakers while he swerved around a disa-

bled beggar. The beggar's coins spilled on the pavement: a hand-
ful of 50 Guinean franc coins, a few euro cents, an Australian
dollar, and a Byzantine gold *nomisma* in the effigy of emperor
Michael IV the Paphlagonian.

"My sister is amazing," said Moon Boké.

"Sounds like it," I said.

"Ehhhhh, you know what's amazing, is that your dad is the
emperor over there in Toronto!" he added. "I can't believe it!
I can't believe it! We're going to make some great contents together! Our enemies will not even understand what is happening to them!"

"I'm glad," I said blankly. My mind was somewhere else, perhaps turned off entirely. I had left my body on autopilot on the
passenger seat of a Guinean SUV charging down the Boulevard
de la Corniche, and it seemed to be doing fine fending for itself
unattended. There was no urgent need to reassociate and return
to the world.

Half of the boulevard was closed off while Anhui Construction Engineering Corporation technicians dug, graded, and
paved all the way from the center to the restaurant. The other
half of the boulevard was essentially unpaved.

The car moved in a series of low-resolution perpendicular
jolts until my spine was square. All my bones were downgraded to their low-res version until my whole body was just a few
bytes. My mind stopped spinning to preserve the contents of
memory.

Finally Moon Boké interrupted:

"We have arrived!"

We sat down facing the ocean. Béatrice promptly ordered three
times fish and rice.

"Did I tell you what happened?" Moon Boké asked.

I smiled without nodding.

"It's so sad. So sad. I was doing so much for that town," he
continued without waiting for my answer. "I was doing everything! I built a hospital and a mosque in Boké. And a maternity

ward. Because young women would just give birth in a ditch. What kind of country are we to allow such a thing, you know?"

I tilted my head slightly.

He continued: "Ah, this country is so corrupt! It's so corrupt. I do infrastructure as a hobby, right? So I was in a meeting with the Minister of Public Works. We want to build a new road, he said. Fine, I said. So give us an invoice for thirty million Guinean francs and we put ten million in your account and split the rest, he said. And in one year we need a little something for the inspector because it's foreign aid money, he said."

"Is that how things work?" I asked.

"Ehhhh, what did you think…." he said, biting off the head of the fish that had just been put in front of him.

"The project was approved, facilities were planned with the financial support of the French Ministry of Cooperation, but the funds disappeared during a power outage, and to this day cannot be located," said Béatrice matter-of-factly while Moon Boké was chewing.

"bye bye," said an ad for bug spray painted on the side of a truck driving by.

"Anyway that man — listen," Moon Boké continued, "his kids go to school in Switzerland. He bought them a container of iPhones as a present. Not a dozen iPhones, but a container! That's 2,660 iPhones. What are the kids going to do with 2,660 iPhones? Even in Switzerland."

"Mhm," I nodded.

"People are fed up. And so they started spreading bad rumors because someone said that something had happened but you know it's like when people say that something is happening only because they're spreading rumors about what's happening because they're fed up, you see?" he asked.

"I see," I said with confidence.

"That's how the riots started. It's so sad. So sad. I was doing so much for that town," he continued. "And they burned several of my Lamborghinis."

"Several?" I asked.

"I kept some of my finest cars in Boké. I love that town. I wanted to do everything for it," he said.

"I totally get it. You wanted to honor it by keeping some of your best Lamborghinis there," I said, looking him in the eye.

"Yes! Yes! You get me!" he said, shaking my hand enthusiastically across the table. "Yes! Thank you!"

"I think I do get you actually, I really do," I said. "You're very much like my father in some ways."

"Ehhhh! Princeeeeessssss! Your father sounds like a good man. We're going to make some great contents together! Some amazing contents! We're going to be the only TV channel in West Africa with Byzantine contents! Our enemies will not even understand what is happening to them!"

I chewed my fish. I remembered the Atlantic at my feet, dark, peripheral, off duty, wrapped around the city like a popped-out balloon.

"This is a good piece of fish for you," he said.

We ate with joy and appetite.

5

The riots in Boké lasted eight years. They followed the ancient rules of the chronodrome™: peanuts are heated over a great fire and mixed with water until peanut goo is obtained. Then a circular clock face is drawn on the ground with a solution of peanut goo, yoghurt, and hair gel, 300 yards in diameter, and that perimeter becomes an inviolable portal space until someone dies. A sharp conical spike, two feet tall and made of rusted iron, is placed in the exact center, with the tip up.

A clock hand, made of one single trunk of palm tree, is brought in, and hinged on the spike in the center.

Then the contestants challenge one another on the chronodrome™.

On one side was Moon Boké, wearing a Baoulé mask and a deep-black magic bogolan, driving four Lamborghinis at once, all of them on fire, leaving a gleaming trail of gold coins and warm pineapple juice, with fluffy pink stuffed rabbits, warthogs, monkeys, shrimp, and lobsters masturbating in his wake and ejaculating molten lead into the sand.

With each revolution around the sacred circle, shrieking crowds of supporters threw showers of pomegranate confetti at their champion until the ground was red and slick and the four fiery Lamborghinis careened like knights of the Apocalypse treading a stream of blood.

On the other side was a 1997 Toyota Corolla, Ibrahima the blind griot in the driver's seat, Seydou the money changer at his side, holding a fine Fouta Djalon lamb in his lap. On the hood of the Toyota was a cow, saved from sacrifice in the hills above Nzérékoré, Nafissatou riding on its back and holding it by the horns, her dark indigo boubou billowing in the wind like a celestial pennant as she roared "Abominable! Abominable!" at the opposing team. In the back, hanging from the tailgate in regal equipoise, was Chantal, holding rats in one hand and an anvil in the other. On the trunk, these hand-painted words: "What do you want?"

All around the sacred perimeter, hundreds of decapitated migrant workers from Burkina Faso stood wraith-like and soundless, risen from the dead, each carrying his head in his arms. With every revolution of the 1997 Toyota Corolla they held up in their head in a silent hosanna, and with every passage of the Lamborghinis they held them up again in a gesture of reproach.

In normal chronodrome™ usage, the competitors have to run at the same speed as the clock hand. If they run faster, they become younger and younger until they are unborn, at which point they lose because they don't exist yet. And if they run slower than the clock hand, time passes them by and they age until they're too tired and they die of old age.

But this was no normal chronodrome™ race. The contestants were driving, not running, and both sides have always existed and neither one has ever gotten tired. The four blazing Lamborghinis ran forever under an inexhaustible flurry of red pomegranates, leaving an endless trail of gold coins, cheered on by an infinite crowd of supporters. At their helm, the Baoulé mask, still and expressionless, its shiny mouthless ebony face gleaming in the fire, its unseeing wooden bulging conical eyes staring ahead yet letting no light pass. The old Toyota Corolla also ran forever, and the decapitated migrant workers never got tired of saluting it silently.

After eight years, seven months, eleven days, six hours, and six minutes, the riots in Boké stopped. The general public went home, made spaghetti bolognese, checked their social media, and forgot about the race. But the contestants didn't stop, and to this day the cosmic battle rages on.

6

In the end, my father won an Oscar for *The Battle of Dyrrachium* at the Constantinople Biennale. It has remained a classic in Byzantine cinema, not just for its epic plot and the unique realism of having thousands of extras slaughtered on camera, but also for its innovative filming and lighting techniques.

It was the first Byzantine film to use wooden lenses: very thin strips of blond cedar, mounted to the front of cylindrical cedar cameras and kept in place by cedar staples. *The Battle of Dyrrachium* required twenty-seven staple guns and thousands of staples just to keep the lenses in place during the shooting. Since wood is opaque, the entire film is completely dark.

Each scene starts in an elevator. The doors open with a little ding, the camera peeks out, giving the audience a first-person perspective. Each time, it is completely dark. There is nothing inside or outside the elevator. Then the doors close again.

The Battle of Dyrrachium was the first Byzantine film to be shot outdoors with three kinds of light, as is now standard everywhere. The key light, or *kleidophos,* was designed out of one single trunk of beech beveled to a point at one end, flattened into a square tray at the other end, and laden with sacks of bronze coins. Since it is dark and produces no illumination, it requires the scene to be simultaneously narrated by an assistant called the *kleidophotologos.* This is usually done by an adolescent virgin girl. If none are available, by a certified accountant. And if none are available, by a boy less than five years old. And if none are available, by a dog or a wild animal.

The fill light, or *plerophos,* was placed opposite the *kleidophos* to prevent single-source darkness from creating sharp contrasts in the scene. It is not actually a light but a very large mirror made of coarsely felted hair lined with green corduroy, placed on a thick foam pad covered in tufted black leatherette, which rotates throughout the day to follow the position of the sun in the sky. Since none of those surfaces are reflective, the *plerophos* is also completely dark.

The kick light, sometimes called back light or *opisthophos,* was placed on Venetian ships in the Dyrrachium harbor to take advantage of the sea's reflective surface. It consists of wooden towers with thick beams cut into large bludgeons studded with sharp iron nails and hoisted to the top of the masts. The *opistho- pos* does not produce any light either, but penetrates enemy flesh like cute pink straws poking into bubble tea or an unsuspecting milkshake — which sometimes is better than good light in terms of cinematography.

For scenes filmed in Africa, the harsh bright light was filtered by diesel haze produced by the Venetian ships' engines, which were left to rev all day to create this special effect. This is why, to this day, in film industry jargon this type of light is called "Venetian diesel," even if nowadays it is often added digitally in post-production.

7

After dinner, I dutifully returned the staple gun to my hotel reception and asked to borrow a pneumatic sledgehammer instead.

"We have two," said the receptionist, "a medium one, which is quite heavy and suitable for breaking pavement, and a huge pneumatic one for heavy demolition work, but it takes several people to move and you won't be able to do it by yourself."

"I'll have the huge one please. I have some heavy demolition work to do. God will send angels to help me carry it, thanks."

I left my credit card as a deposit and the receptionist handed me the huge pneumatic sledgehammer from behind the desk. Then God sent four angels to help me carry it, as Moïse had predicted while slurping cow meat.

They descended from the sky on a Chinese-made moped in a cloud of blue exhaust smoke and parked in front of the reception desk. Moïse himself was driving, behind him the second angel carried a big cross made of two PVC plumbing tubes covered in Manchester United stickers. At the back of the moped the third angel stood on the saddle, brandishing a cassette tape player blasting a 1980s Madonna album at full volume. The fourth angel sat on the third angel's shoulders, holding a banner that read: "The Trumpet Shall Sound."

"Oh I recognize you," I said to Moïse's three companions, "you made me fish that night in that dark alley in Ségou, and brought me a little stool to sit on!"

They smiled and winked silently. We filed into the elevator and went to the top floor of the hotel, carrying the pneumatic sledgehammer together. The elevator was a bit rickety, a few buttons and masks were missing and the pomegranate dispenser was broken.

The doors opened with a little ding. I peeked out. Because the elevator was a supernatural portal, we were on the roof of the market in Ségou, and also on the roof of my hotel in Conakry, and also on the roof the Blachernae Palace in Constantinople, and on the roof of the basilica in Yamoussoukro. All those buildings had the same roof after all, and perhaps that is one of the morals of this story. Many buildings in the world actually have the same roof, just different elevators — -and most of the time you have to take the stairs anyway.

Trans time travelers have a fraught relationship with elevators. We live in elevators, but they're rancid claustrophobic boxes — sometimes made of hair — that smell of lightly worn underwear. We can't even press the buttons without opening strange portals and summoning dark spirits, and just going up and down involves wielding a staple gun and figuring out the motivations of the charismatic straight men who have fought over it. And yet, through technology and poetic imagination, we keep alive the prospect of our rancid box opening up onto a gentle utopia that is always moments away from becoming real.

But fine: now I had four angels with me, I was finally on the roof, the doors had opened up, things were going to get real.

I proceeded to my business. In my pocket I found a concave *hyperpyron* coin in the effigy of my father Emperor Alexios, made of a dirty alloy of gold, silver, tin, rats, mayonnaise, hair, and other stuff. I placed it on the bare concrete floor and the angels helped me lift the huge pneumatic sledgehammer over it.

Then, speaking aloud the name of my savior Jesus Christ in this final liturgical moment, I aimed the tip of the pneumatic sledgehammer at my father's imperial face, crushed it with a thunderous bang, and obliterated any trace of his likeness.

bye bye

The impact made it warm to the touch — finally. The coin was no longer a coin, but a variegated nugget of mottled metal with a subdued twinkle. It couldn't be exchanged anymore: so long, transactional sparkle.

"So, that's that," said Moïse. "I think we're all done here."

A demon had been made homeless in this metallic exorcism — it used to dwell in that little metal idol and cavort in my pocket as a black sabbath venue for the Empire. But see, currency is not inescapable and can be taken out of circulation.

The angels left and I remained alone. For a moment I felt no relief and I looked for the familiar shackles of queer self-doubt. Perhaps I had just been one more Byzantine princess with an outburst of iconoclasm?

In the year 695, when Emperor Justinian II minted coins with a human effigy on the obverse, our Muslim neighbors — who until then had gladly used our Byzantine currency in their own affairs — took exception, and their caliph Abd al-Malik denounced the practice as idolatry. Now I was beginning to think that the Muslims were right. Was I betraying my family and my country for siding with the enemy? Was that unbecoming of a purple-born Byzantine princess, and of the propriety required by my rank?

The breeze picked up and blew a plastic bag into my face. I cleared it away and proclaimed the advent of the moxie time-traveling queer dynasty of just me. The game was over. I wasn't going to be disowned by a man whose face I had just crushed with a pneumatic sledgehammer — thanks.

God, it turns out, has infinite mercy and loans out power tools to those who need them. I had put them to good use in this book, bearing witness to the transfiguration of Christ and to my own, and defeating the demon that had presumed to stand between me and my Designer.

Now it was bright, sunny, and windy, and I was surrounded by plastic trash. The clouds were moving fast. My dress billowed around my legs in furious golden whorls and made me feel like a radiant 3D Marilyn Monroe popping out of a Byzantine mosaic with halo and all. My acquaintance the seagull gracefully flew across the horizon, triumphantly raising a piece of fresh rotten something into the sun. This was my new home: a cloud of trash in the sky, windy and fresh, beyond every elevator, beyond hair and masks, free and exposed to the cosmos and the giggling stars.

The sky was deep, intense, and saturated. It dunked into the rough ocean below my feet and dissolved there in a great jamboree of blue and yellow — only God's own celestial brand of indigo was water-soluble. I saw that the boundary between the sky and the sea was hazy and indistinct and made of the same substance as my blood: watery sand — malleable, liquid, fluid.

I now pronounce my imperial biography concluded. I declare myself not a chronicler, but a hymnographer, and this book the first hymn of the new liturgy. Amen.

Made in United States
North Haven, CT
11 May 2025

68717519R00108